KYFF

Equestrian Fiction by Barbara Morgenroth

Bittersweet Farm 1: Mounted
Bittersweet Farm 2: Joyful Spirit
Bittersweet Farm 3: Wingspread
Bittersweet Farm 4: Counterpoint
Bittersweet Farm 5: Calling All Comets
Bittersweet Farm 6: Kyff
Bittersweet Farm 7: Lyric Line
Bittersweet Farm 8: Tea Biscuit
Bittersweet Farm 9: Roll the Dice
Bittersweet Farm 10: Whiskey Tango
Bittersweet Farm 11: Partial Stranger
Bittersweet Farm 12: Available
Bittersweet Farm 13: Knock Knock

If Wishes Were Horses   a novella

Middle-grade

Dream Horse
Summer Horse

BITTERSWEET FARM 6

KYFF

Barbara Morgenroth

DashingBooks

Bittersweet Farm 6: Kyff © 2014
Barbara Morgenroth
http://barbaramorgenroth.com

This is a work of fiction. While references may be made to actual places or events, all names, characters, incidents and locations are from the author's imagination and do not resemble any actual living or dead persons, businesses, or events.

Any similarity is coincidental.

ISBN 978-0692303542

Cover photo by Radelukovic
Published by DashingBooks
Text set in Adobe Garamond

JANUARY

IT WAS NEW YEAR'S DAY and snowing again. The house that seemed empty would soon be full of people but that wouldn't fill the void. Family should be together at significant moments and while this was just a date on a calendar, January 1 was still a time for reflection on the past as well as for looking forward into the future.

Greer and Lockie should have been here at the farm in Connecticut, not fifteen hundred miles away in Florida surrounded by strangers. They would be at Teche Chartier's two-day open house party held at the farm in Napier and all the riders, trainers and owners preparing for the winter show circuit would be there. It would be like any Teche gathering, partly Cajun, partly New Orleanian, and completely extravagant. He had caterers flown in from

Louisiana to insure the guests were getting an authentic experience.

Our party seemed quite modest in comparison and I hoped the snow would make it even more so. Jules and I had cooked for two days, making amuse-bouches, verrines, small desserts, and pink champagne truffles. The only help we had was Caprice, whose mother owned a restaurant, and knew her way around a kitchen almost as well as she knew her way around the barn.

I wasn't in the mood for a party or guests but my attendance was required as we all needed to lend a hand. We didn't have people come in to serve or clean up. These were things we did as a family. Some might have called it an episode of temporary insanity but having an open house was how we celebrated New Year's Day.

Jules and I had bought matching midnight blue velvet dresses and had spent an afternoon attaching gold sequins in the shape of stars on them. We had gold star earrings and I had the Bittersweet Farm necklace my father and Jules had given me for Christmas. Even though it went against the star theme, it was important to me.

When I went downstairs, Jules already had soft jazz playing on the sound system.

"Smile, Dolcezza," she said to me.

"This should have been my first New Year's celebration with Lockie," I replied. "These days are the ones you remember. They stand out because they're not a commonplace day. I won't remember November 14 in ten years but I will remember that this was a day we weren't together."

Jules put her arm around me. "My father traveled a great deal when I was a child. He travels still. He missed birthdays and holidays."

"Then you understand."

She laughed. "I do but I don't."

I sighed.

"If you have the kind of job that requires you to be away from home, either the family accepts that or you find something else to do."

The oven timer began dinging and we walked into the kitchen together to begin plating the little noshes that were cooked to perfection. There were miniature breadsticks to be dipped in black truffle and chablis mustard, bite-size custard tarts with asparagus, phyllo dough purses stuffed with artichoke and goat cheese and the first half sheet of airy gougères. These would go quickly, but we were prepared with several dozen more in the freezer in case of an amuse-bouche emergency.

Cap came through the door wearing a red cocktail dress, barn coat and knee high insulated winter boots, carrying her party shoes in a plastic shopping bag. We had suggested getting dressed at the house made sense but she wanted to give the horses a look and get ready at her apartment.

"I heard from Mill." She pulled off the boots. "It's eighty degrees with blue, cloudless skies and there are a dozen people in the swimming pool."

I looked at Jules.

"Sounds like Los Angeles." Jules began to put a small bit of pâté we had made yesterday inside the gougères, then held one out to me.

I took a bite. "Delicious."

Jules passed one over to Cap.

"Did Mill mention Lockie?" I asked.

"No. I think we spoke for all of about three minutes as he was just about to start a game of polo. He's very impressed with Teche's ponies."

"When does Mill have to get back to college?" Jules asked as she arranged the noshes on a platter then began sprinkling pomegranate seeds around them.

"Soon," Cap said. "I don't know if he'll even come back to Newbury or just fly back to California."

Jules and I shared a look.

The doorbell rang.

"I'll get it," Cap offered.

"Thank you. I'm sure Andrew will be downstairs in a minute," Jules replied.

"I'll go see what's keeping him," I said and left the kitchen followed by Joly, Greer's puppy.

Upstairs, I tapped on my father's door. "Dad."

"Come in, Tal."

I opened the door and we entered. He was wearing the vest Greer and I had given him for Christmas, a handmade needlepoint depiction of the farm.

"Guests are beginning to arrive," I said.

"I was working." He pointed to his desk. "This is going to be a very busy year for me. An important year."

"I know." I reached down and gave Joly's head a pat. "Maybe we'll be able to help you. I'm not very well organized...but Greer is."

"She is, isn't she?" He smiled.

My sister had managed the Ambassador of Good Cheer Project without much input from me. She had a hidden talent for coordinating schedules and keeping details straight while for me such things tended to become a tangle like a skein of wool that had tied itself in knots.

"I'll do what I can," I replied.

"I'm sure you will. Just do what you're doing. Maybe later in the year Amanda will get you started."

Amanda was our teacher who had homeschooled us and was now at the farm to teach Greer how to run a charity. I was relegated to what I did best—working in the barn. That was my speed, my area of expertise such as it was.

"Let's start the New Year without dwelling on the past or fretting about our insufficiencies." My father put his arm around my shoulders. "We'll do better as we go along."

I nodded.

"You didn't think I could do as well as I did last year," he teased.

"I was shocked until I realized you were just copying your own father," I teased back as we went down the hallway.

"He's a grandfather now. Don't confuse him with the man he was when I was a child."

I paused at the top of the stairs. "Is that true?"

"Ask him yourself." My father smiled.

"Talia!" Grandfather Shay called from the bottom of the stairs and extended his arms to me.

I hurried to him and received a crushing hug.

"I thought you were traveling," I said.

"We came here to stay for a while."

"Here here?" I asked in confusion.

"Here. Some of the time when your grandmother and I aren't staying in the city."

I thought for a moment. "Is the business in trouble?"

My father came up behind me. "No. You're not to worry about Swope."

"I'm a little bored," my grandfather said, "and your father has other demands to manage."

"Do you want us around all the time telling you what to eat and what to wear?" My grandmother came up alongside me and planted a kiss on my cheek.

"Yes," I replied.

My grandparents laughed because they thought I was kidding.

***

The afternoon progressed to the sound of jazz, conversation and much laughter. Many trays and platters of food were brought to the guests, then returned to the kitchen dotted with a few crumbs. After the freezer was raided for more gougères, we unwrapped another disk of Coulommiers cheese since the first one disappeared quickly. A case of empty bottles of sparkling peach juice was pushed to the side and a case of raspberry opened.

There were friends of my father, neighbors and of course Pavel, Danuta and Tomasz in the living room. Poppy and Aly stopped by and helped with some of the mess being made. Our friends from the animal shelter arrived in time to greet the Meades, although Oliver stayed home, which was for the best because everyone seemed to be entertained enough.

I waited for Jos and Brad Deering to turn up but they never did. When I had invited her, Jos had expressed more doubt than enthusiasm and it made me wonder how difficult it was for her. Having had a problematic home life of my own, I could only hope this year would be an improvement for her. There wasn't much I could do if her father didn't want to cooperate.

By the time the day slipped into a winter's late afternoon, the guests left and Cap and I changed in order to do the barn. We came back to the house for a light dinner, all that was desired after noshing most of the day.

I went upstairs early because all I wanted to do was sit in bed with Joly at my side and read for a while.

My phone rang.

"My cover is blown," Greer said.

"How did they find out?"

"Victoria Kensington-Rowe couldn't keep it to herself."

"I thought you told your mother not to say anything."

"It wasn't entirely her fault. Teche made a big deal about it. 'Her book is nearly as hot as my spice mix'."

"Okay. How did you get linked to your mother?"

"She put her arm around me and called me her 'darling daughter'."

We had decided it would be necessary to lay down some ground rules for her mother when Victoria turned up in Florida. She was not to tell anyone she and Greer were related. Victoria said she understood. Shame on us for believing her.

"I'm sorry."

"Me, too. *Tight Chaps and Loose Tarts* is climbing the charts and picking up speed," Greer said in resignation. "How's Joly?"

"He's right here with me and was a gentleman this afternoon."

"Well. The good part is we're done with the holidays."

"True. Have a good night."

"Talk to you tomorrow."

By the time I said goodbye, she was gone. Greer needed an upgrade in the phone manners department.

I shut off my tablet and turned out the light. "Don't pee on the bed," I told Joly. "If you have to go out, wake me up."

He snuggled closer so that I had no room at all.

My phone rang.

"Were you still up?"

"Barely," I replied.

"I'm sorry," Lockie said. "I won't interrupt you."

"I was waiting for you to call."

"You could have called me."

I had learned early on that when my father was busy conducting business he wasn't to be interrupted. Lockie was in Florida on business. If he was training Greer or riding a horse or speaking with a potential customer, his phone shouldn't be a distraction. Of course, he could turn it off, but that wasn't the point of having a phone. It was better to leave the casual conversations to off-hours. Unfortunately, I had no way of knowing which hours those were.

"You were at Teche's gala weren't you?"

"That was yesterday night. Tonight I was in the barn with Cam. One of the horses has some heat in one of his hind legs, so we were taking care of that."

"Is he going to be okay?"

"We'll get the vet out tomorrow to check him over."

"Being a veterinarian must be the best job in town at the moment," I said.

"They're all busier than a horse fly on the winter show circuit," Lockie replied. "Someone's at my door. I'd better go see who it is. Go to sleep, Talia. Goodnight."

"Talk to you tomorrow." I don't know if he heard me because, like Greer, Lockie was gone, too.

I put the phone back on the nightstand. "Joly, it's turning out to be a good thing that Greer left you here with me."

2

ON JANUARY FOURTH, they packed up early and headed for Wynyard, Florida. So said the text message Greer left for me, which only made me feel twice as removed from them than if I had been able to speak to her or Lockie. There were a dozen horses going from Teche's farm, Acadiana South, and it had to be almost as involved as moving an army from one location to another. I had found taking two horses in the van to a show in-state to be complicated enough but this was beyond my imagination.

By the time I got down to the barn, Cap looked to be in the same kind of mood I was in.

"I heard from Mill," she said.

"That's more than I got."

"Surprise! He's going to Argentina."

"What? What's in Argentina?"

11

"A string of Teche's polo ponies." Cap rested the manure fork on the floor. "Mill's taking a sabbatical from school."

"You can cry in front of me, I won't think less of you," I replied.

"My life has prepared me for being blindsided," she said. "Teche is being very generous and will cover the tuition for UConn when Mill gets back to Connecticut."

"It is a well-respected agricultural university," I admitted but had no idea if it was as excellent as California Polytechnic.

"The family farm is in California. Cal Poly is just up the highway." She picked up the fork. "So I guess I'll go home."

"If Mill is going to be working for Teche, do you want to be on the West Coast when he's out here? Stay at Bittersweet."

"In a month, Tracy will be back. This is her job and I don't want to be a usurper."

Thanks, Mill, for throwing your girlfriend's life into turmoil.

"We have the additional stalls, you're needed if you'd like to stay."

"It's Tracy's apartment."

"That's something we can work out. Think about it. If you want to stay, you're more than welcome. Have...your horse—"

"Bijou," Cap supplied.

"That's his name. Have him sent out to be with you here. Everyone should be with their horse."

Cap turned to the stall then turned back. "I know this is an excellent opportunity for Mill. He loves playing polo, but this is just not what we had planned."

"You're still working with horses. Maybe you hate New Newbury."

She smiled. "No, but after being uprooted from Connecticut and having to get used to California, I thought I was staying there."

"I understand."

I did. But not all surprises turn out to be unpleasant.

***

Just after lunch, Jos arrived.

"A neighbor gave me a ride," she said not looking at me.

"Okay. Go get Foxy and put him on the cross ties so have a look at him. Hold onto him when you lead him."

Jos nodded and went outside.

About three minutes later Foxy trotted into the barn without her.

I shook my head at Cap. "He does that when he thinks he can get away with it. A big joke to him."

"He does look pleased with himself," she replied.

Jos ran in. "Sorry."

"Next time you'll be prepared," Cap said as she went to get Spare for his exercise session.

My phone started ringing, so I checked it and headed for the tack room. "Hi."

"Hi. We're in Wynyard," Lockie said.

"It's that far?"

"No, but it takes that long when one of the tires falls off a gooseneck trailer."

This wasn't good. "Was anyone hurt?"

"No, but it was a mess trying to get it fixed," Lockie replied.

"Was it the trailer with Counterpoint?"

"No. I did not have to deal with a hysterical Greer," Lockie said.

"Is she okay?"

"Greer's riding beautifully. If she maintains that level of performance, she should do well this weekend." Lockie paused for a moment. "What should I expect if she doesn't win? Is she going to have a melt-down?"

I thought about it for a moment. "Do you care about her?"

"Yes."

"Not as your student, but as a person."

"Of course I do. She's your sister."

"Then you're thinking of it backwards."

"How so?"

"Don't react to her. Don't deal with her. Don't handle her. Care about her. She'll be fine."

"Okay." He sounded doubtful.

"Don't worry about the swish."

"Are you revealing your training secrets?"

"Only to you," I replied.

"I'd better go. I still have three horses to school before the sun goes down. I'll call you tonight. Is that good?"

"Very good. Say goodbye, don't just click off."

Lockie laugh. "Goodbye, Talia."

"Goodbye, Lockie."

There was a pause. "Now we hang up?"

"Yes."

"Bye."

I slid my phone back in my pocket and was just about to step out of the tack room when Cap came in.

"Am I interrupting?"

"No. That was the mid-afternoon Florida update."

She sat on a tack trunk. "They're good?"

I nodded.

"I had an idea. It's a little bit out there but it could work."

"If you think we're strangers to things being a little out there, you haven't been here long enough. Stick around."

"I don't have much choice. I don't think Mill is ever going back to Cal Poly. He called me earlier, so excited about working with Teche's polo string. My bet is that he'll stay here and go to UConn if he even goes back to school."

"He's had a great opportunity handed to him but this isn't like working at a hack stable. This is a pretty good opportunity for you, too," I replied.

"It wasn't meant to detract from Bittersweet," Cap said quickly.

"I didn't take it that way, don't think twice about it. Now what's this idea you've had?"

"People make videos and put them on viewtube."

"Yes, we've watched some of Cam Rafferty's rounds at big shows that way."

"People demonstrate how to knit, or frost cakes, or do things on the computer," Cap said.

"I guess they do."

"Foxy got away from Jos earlier. There must be more than a couple kids new to riding, or just got a pony and they don't know the basics. Foxy took advantage of her lack of experience."

"He sure did."

"Let's make a video for pony riders and show kids how to correctly lead a pony."

I shook my head. "I'm sorry. I'm not following you. What good would that do?"

"It's the middle of the winter. It'll give us something to do while everyone has abandoned us and kids might find it on viewtube, watch it and learn something."

"Just the one video?"

"Start with one. The second one could be..." Cap started to laugh, "how to pick out a hoof without using a pry bar to get it off the floor."

I started to laugh. "Garter shifts all his weight to the leg you're trying to work on."

"I had a pony who knew when you were going around back and he'd snap you in the face with his tail."

"I love them but they are little monsters, aren't they?"

"Ponytude," Cap said.

"That's a good name for it," I replied. "I don't know anything about videos and the camera went with Greer to Florida."

"Problem," Cap admitted. "Wait. There was a guy a couple years ahead of me in Old Newbury High—"

"They have a high school so far out in the wilderness?"

"Yes, it was a one-room schoolhouse, just like in good old colony times. Wayne and his brother Wayne."

"What?"

"It's a blended family with really bad naming luck. They called one Wayne and the other Waynie."

"Sheesh."

"They wanted to be independent filmmakers and were always doing crazy stuff like acting out plays where everyone was a huge vegetable. They have a good sense of..."

"Humor?"

"No. It's more surreal than that. They're the Salvador Dalis of video. If they're still around, we could talk to them. They know everything about digital."

"We don't want the kids to look like giant carrots," I said. "Some pony will get the wrong idea."

Cap found the phone book in the desk drawer. "No. We'll explain that the Waynes have to be dull and uncreative about it."

***

That afternoon, we drove into the wilds of Connecticut to meet the Waynes at their small studio and they were not what I expected. Not that I had a good track-record at picturing people before I met them. I had been spectacularly wrong about Lockie.

"Hi," Wayne said as he opened the door. "I remember you," he said to Cap.

"Why would you?" she asked quite sensibly.

"You always looked like you just came in from working the fields while all the other girls looked like they were trying to impress guys," a Wayne replied.

"My entire high school experience described in one sentence," Cap said to me.

"It must have been different for you that last year in California," I replied.

"No, it was the same thing, except that since riding was a valid PE course, I was not the only one with manure on her boots."

"You need a video job done?" the Wayne at the computer asked.

"We just want to record a short video. No artistic statements," Cap said.

"How short?"

"Five minutes," I replied.

"Definitely under ten," Cap said. "We want it simple and straight-forward. We want to be talking as we do the demonstration."

"So you don't want to do a voice-over?" the other Wayne asked.

I looked at Cap.

"Narrate it after it's shot," the Wayne at the computer explained.

"We don't want it to complicate our lives," I replied. "Come to the farm, do your thing and then we upload it to viewtube."

A Wayne smiled. "We'd have to edit it. Put a title on it. Cut it so that it plays well. Add music at the beginning and end."

Cap shook her head. "I didn't realize so much had to be done. It sounds expensive."

"I'm sure you're worth whatever you charge but we don't want a production. We just want to illustrate one thing."

"Come over here and look at what we'd do for you," the Wayne at the computer said.

We went closer to the huge monitor and in a moment, a video began playing. There was music, a title, a commercial for regional technical school and then the closing.

"Businesses need commercials to let people know they exist. This will run on the television station in Bridgeport."

I didn't realize there was one, but I didn't watch much television.

"It's not art but it helps pay the bills," the other Wayne said. "We're film makers."

"Artists," his brother added.

"That looked fine to me. How much do you charge?" I asked.

Cap was handed a price sheet and my phone began to ring.

"Excuse me," I said and, stepping to the other side of the room, I clicked it on. "Hi."

"Hi. Are you done with chores?" Lockie asked.

"Yes, but we're not at the barn, we're at a studio talking to a video production team."

"Why?"

"Cap had an idea to help beginning riders manage their ponies."

"Great. Ask the videographers to come to the barn and do a sales video of Sora."

Sora was a horse in training who had been sent to us to get started around Thanksgiving. I didn't think the horse was nearly far enough along but maybe it had become a "must sell" situation for the owner.

"Okay. I'll ask. Who is supposed to show the horse to sell it?"

"You and Cap. I'm not there."

What I knew about selling horses could fit into a teaspoon so Lockie must have been talking about Cap more than me.

"Alright."

"Talk to you later."

"Say bye."

"Bye."

"Bye."

I think he clicked off after the conversation ended.

3

OVER DINNER, Cap and I explained Lockie's request to do a video sales pitch for Sora and our own instructional video on the correct way to lead a pony to my father. We had spent time before dinner, determining a ballpark price based on the numbers the Waynes had given us and it was reasonable.

My father told us to go ahead with the understanding he approve of the videos before we went public with them. Jules thought super short instructional videos would be perfect for young riders with short attention spans and asked what other topics we would cover.

I didn't want to disappoint her, but one was probably going to stretch us to the limit.

It would have been terrific to have a video of Trish and Oliver performing but maybe there would be an opportunity for Valentine's Day since we had talked about scheduling a few visits for that holiday. Without Greer being at home, it was difficult to juggle the Ambassador of Good Cheer with everything else that needed to be done. I hoped the process would become more streamlined as the month went along but I doubted it. Even with the help Teche had sent from his barn, there was a limit to how many horses Cap and I could ride in one day. And neither of us were Lockie. He was a real trainer, we were just riders.

Cap and I took Joly out for his evening constitutional then she went back to her apartment and I went up to my room wondering if I had just gotten in way over my head. It was one thing managing the barn on my own, but to try to sell horses and make an instructional video was like nothing I had ever done before. Both carried risks of being personally and professionally embarrassed and I explained the situation to Joly as I got ready for bed. He watched as I moved around the room and seemed to be paying attention.

My phone rang and I had to dig it out of my jeans pocket. Fortunately, it hadn't made it into the laundry due to my inability to remember all the details of my life.

"Hi, how are you?" I asked.

"I want to tell you something," Greer said.

Her tone of voice conveyed how serious this was.

Not one more thing today.

"Okay. What happened?"

"It's about Lockie."

My brain stopped working for a moment.

"I didn't hug him back. It's not like when I played that joke on you. This happened and I don't want anyone else telling you."

"Greer—."

"—We had just gotten through our last training session. I dismounted, he hugged me and said I did a nice job."

It sounded pretty tame to me. I sat on the bed and put my spare hand on Joly.

"Don't be mad at me," Greer said quickly, "I'm sure it didn't mean anything."

"It meant you did a good job and he likes you."

"Why would he like me?"

"There are so many reasons."

"I've been such a bitch to him."

"I called him an idiot so I wasn't sunshine and cupcakes either. Lockie is very forgiving and what's in the past is best left there. Go forward."

"My first class is tomorrow," she said.

"I know how I'd feel about that. How do you feel?"

"You..." Greer sighed. "I don't want to disappoint anyone. We came a long way to do this."

"That's true. You're going to be in a class with riders from all over the country. Most of them won't place. It's a statistics thing. Everyone doesn't win."

"But, people expect more of me."

"That's where you're wrong. None of us expect anything from you except your best effort. Everyone has good days. Everyone has bad days. Same for Counterpoint. Maybe he gets up on the wrong side of the stall tomorrow morning. Maybe a kid lets a balloon go just as he's crossing the starting line, he thinks it's a pterodactyl out to get him and he shies. It doesn't have anything to do with you."

"But if I was a good rider, I would overcome the balloon."

"No."

"Lockie would overcome the helium balloon," Greer insisted.

"Lockie can't make CB stop doing his swish. I rest my case. They're horses not motorbikes. They have emotions and thoughts of some kind. Maybe Counterpoint doesn't feel like jumping tomorrow and maybe CB feels like doing the cha-cha. You can't do anything but laugh it off."

"I'm the one who's supposed to know how to make the best of a bad situation," Greer replied.

"That's what you keep telling me. What time is the class? I'll watch the streaming online coverage."

"One. Right after the lunch break."

"Okay. Wave to me. I'll wave back."

"What if that's when the kid lets go of the balloon?"

"Yeah. Just sit there and be a passenger. Now, I've got a situation and need your help. See there are these two guys named Wayne..."

25

***

Nearly asleep when my phone rang, I felt for it on my nightstand and seeing the ID clicked it on.

"Hi. I heard you've been hugging on Greer."

There was a pause.

"She confessed."

"I did," Lockie said. "This winter series seems so important to her. I don't want her to transmit her tension to Counterpoint. Was she always this conflicted about showing?"

"Not that I noticed but I was usually in a pretty bad mood anyway. I know she doesn't want to disappoint you."

"Me? Have I put pressure on her?"

"No."

"For all the showing you have done, neither of you seems to understand the exercise. It's a competition. That means there are winners and losers. Over the course of anyone's career they lose more than they win."

"Not Nicole Boisvert."

"She's here. Good luck to her. She's riding in ami-owner hunters against Molly Pinchot who's been doing this for about twice as long as Nicole is old. Nicole won't be able to get around her. That's life in the big ring. Experience counts."

"What about you?"

26

"On the right horse, the right day, everyone can get lucky. The point is to make your horse the right horse and that day the right day. The harder you work, the luckier you get."

"When are you coming home?" I missed him so much it was becoming physically uncomfortable.

"Silly, I'm working on getting luckier."

***

As the week progressed, the weather wasn't going to improve but predicted to get worse, so Cap and I spoke to the Waynes and decided to do the sales video for Sora and the Ponytude video on the same day. Greer had emailed me a detailed outline of what we needed to cover and over almond, chocolate and orange biscotti crisps and tea, Cap, Jules and I attempted to flesh out dialog. We were never going to be able to remember lines like Cam probably could, but as long as we knew what points we had to get across, the shoot should be considered a success.

We asked Aly if Poppy would like to be our video victim but unfortunately she had an appointment that afternoon. Gincy was involved with an afterschool activity so that left Jos, who was the least experienced pony rider we had available to us.

There wasn't much choice. It was go with Jos or have the Waynes come to the farm later in the month and go through all the hassle of setting up equipment again. We asked Jos and she said yes.

Cap and I decided to do several rehearsals with Jos even though she had been good with handling Comet. We weren't using him because he was a little ouchy, so we were using Foxy. Garter was a shaggy mess and Remington was clipped so it would be unfair to take the blanket off him and make him stand outside for an unknowable amount of time while we tried to finish the shoot. Foxy's winter coat was always sleek, and he looked sharp. If Jos did what she was told, and everything went according to plan, there would be no problems.

When was that ever the case at the farm?

***

While the Waynes set up, Cap mounted and we practiced. Cap would walk, trot and canter Sora and I would describe the breeding and training level. There would be some basic dressage, leg yielding, voltes and changes of pace with a halt. Then a few fences would be jumped, and it would be over. We hoped it would take no more than five minutes.

28

It had already taken a couple hours to prepare and I had to raid what was left over in Greer's makeup stash. I was assured that in the middle of the winter, our faces would be mottled bright red and if we didn't use foundation to even out our skin tone, we'd look blotchy. Not wanting that, we applied the makeup and felt like we were wearing spackle. I made a mental note to take girl lessons from Greer when she got home.

After a microphone was clipped to my jacket, the sound was tested and found to be excellent, and my feet were freezing after standing around for so long.

"Okay. We're ready," the Waynes called out to us.

The first thing that happened was Sora shied at the camera on the tripod. Cap let her approach and inspect it thoroughly.

"Stop the horse from breathing on the lens," a Wayne said. "Now it's all fogged up."

We waited for it to clear then began again. The camera was focused on me as I made the brief introduction to Bittersweet Farm and explained that this very nice, young warmblood was for sale.

I felt relieved when the camera was focused on Sora and could narrate off my notes instead of trying to remember what I was supposed to say. Cap did the basic dressage test as I described the training program. With that finished, she popped over a low fence a few times, going back and forth, then took four larger fences to demonstrate the mare's scope and good form.

As Cap returned to a walk, I gave the closing notes and we were done.

"Could you jump the bigger fences again and we'll go in for a close-up," a Wayne requested. "The voice-over was fine, you don't have to do that again."

Cap jumped the bigger fences again, then again so a shot from very low could be done. Sora shied at having a monster crouched near the standard and it took four times before that maneuver was accomplished.

Then we were done with the sales video and Cap went to the barn to leave Sora with Pavel, while I discussed the editing details with the Waynes. A few minutes later, Jos and Cap appeared leading Foxy.

I had emailed the Waynes the script, such as it was, for this Ponytude video so they knew exactly what was supposed to happen. Again, I was going to narrate and Cap was going to demonstrate. Then Jos would follow the instructions and show other pony riders exactly how to lead their mounts. We estimated the video would be about three minutes long since it was simple and straightforward.

"Could we do this outside?" a Wayne asked. "It's dark in the building and this will be a change of scene."

Cap and I looked at each other.

"Seems okay to me," she said.

"Do what we told you to do, Jos," I said to her.

Jos nodded. "I understand."

"Watch Cap show you how it's done and then do exactly the same thing."

"Yes."

Each Wayne had a camera and would shoot the action from a different angle. Cap would walk Foxy in a straight line then make a circle so the audience would be able to see exactly how to lead their ponies. Then it would be Jos's turn.

We began, I started the narration. "You'll stand at your pony's head on the near side. Hold the lead rope with your right hand about twelve inches from the halter."

Cap demonstrated.

"Do not wrap the lead rope around your hand. Hold the rest of the rope in your left hand. You may double it over so it's not dragging on the ground but you do not wrap it around your left hand. You walk forward."

Cap took a step and Foxy followed her.

"Stay alongside your pony's neck. Don't let him pick up the pace so you get behind his shoulder."

Cap slowed up slightly, dropping back so that she was in the wrong position.

"If your pony picks up speed, say whoa and give him a little tug on the lead rope to get his attention."

Cap showed how that was done.

"Not letting go of the lead rope, you can push your hand against your pony's neck if you feel he's turning too close to you."

Cap pushed her hand against Foxy's neck to move him to the right.

"To halt, say whoa and stop walking. Your pony should stop next to you."

Cap and Foxy halted.

The Waynes stopped recording as Cap brought Foxy over to Jos.

"You understand what to do?" I asked.

"I know how to lead a horse," she replied taking the rope.

"Yes, you do. Stay alert. There's a lot going on in the yard. The wind's blowing. Small circle and we're done."

Cap leaned over to me. "He's fine. She can do it."

I nodded.

"Now Jos will demonstrate the proper way to lead a pony."

Jos followed the plan perfectly. Unfortunately, Foxy wasn't so clued in and the moment they rounded the circle, he began to pick up his pace.

"Pull him back," I called.

She was already behind his shoulder and there was nothing she could do to get him under control. He picked up the pace of his trot as Jos struggled to keep up.

"Let him go," I called to her.

She tried to brace herself against him and that only caused her to ski along behind on the snowy side of the driveway.

"Cool," a Wayne said. "Are you getting this?"

"I sure am!" his brother shouted back.

"Let him go!" I shouted into the wind.

"Episode One. How not to lead your pony," Cap commented as Jos gave up.

Finally free, Foxy cantered to the field where Butch and Garter were watching, fascinated, with their heads over the fence.

4

We collected Foxy, and after three attempts managed to get one version where Jos didn't look as though she was going to go skijoring again. The Waynes agreed to drop her off at home and we hurried to the house with only minutes to spare before Greer's class was to begin.

After a quick clean up, we sat at the kitchen table with lunch and the laptop in front of us. The live streaming video of the class hadn't begun.

My phone rang. I checked it and clicked it on.

"Why are you calling me?"

"I'm in the stable area," Greer said.

"Why aren't you warming up? When are you going?"

"An hour from now. Here's Lockie."

There was silence for a moment.

"Hi."

"Is everything okay?"

"There are about fifty horses in this class, we're almost at the end of the line. The forecast is for showers any time now," he said. "What did you do this morning?"

"We did the Sora sales shoot and then Foxy ran off with Jos skiing behind him for the how to lead your pony video."

Lockie laughed too enthusiastically.

"It's not funny. We were freezing out there and Foxy took advantage of her."

"That was predictable. Garter looks like a normal pony and he wouldn't have exceeded the speed limit."

"Garter looks like the puff ball of horse hair and hay you find behind the tack trunks in the spring."

"When is the Sora video going to be ready?"

"Is there a rush?" I asked.

"Yes, I have someone who is interested."

With a deeply overcast sky, the class started and the first horse entered the ring.

"I'll tell the Waynes to go faster."

"Upload a rough cut to viewtube and make it private," Lockie said.

"I'll call them and call you back. Do you know the class has started?"

Lockie laughed. "Yes. We have a PA system here. I'll go get Greer ready. Do you have anything else you want to say to her?"

"Tell her thank you for the help with the videos," I replied.

"Will do. Talk to you later." Lockie paused. "Here's where I say goodbye. Bye."

"Bye." I put the phone on the table. "We have about forty-nine horses to watch before Greer goes."

"Which one of us sits here until number 40 goes and sends up a signal flare?" Cap asked.

"I will. I have a couple phone calls to make," I said.

Cap left for the barn and I picked up the phone as Jules went back to the kitchen area.

"*Paglia e fieno* for dinner?" Jules asked.

"In honor of Greer's debut as an adult rider?"

"Yes." She took the eggs and fresh spinach out of the refrigerator in order to make the yellow and green pasta.

"Is Dad going to be home?"

"He assured me he would be. There was a business meeting with your grandfather that couldn't be postponed."

"Do they know Greer is riding this afternoon?"

"I believe so but you could call and leave a message if he's in conference and can't talk."

"Good suggestion."

"Then you can help me with the pasta. The spinach has to cook first so you have about ten minutes."

"Can you set the timer for about 40 minutes, so we are alerted to Greer's round?"

"Sure can."

I picked up the phone and began making calls.

By the time 30 minutes had passed, the pasta was resting in the refrigerator, and we were all seated at the table with tea and butter cookies watching the monitor as the horses jumped the course in the rain. It wasn't showers, it was a downpour. There were technical problems and the camera lens was spotted with water.

"Some live feeds give you the order of the riders who are waiting to go," Cap commented.

"Not this one," I replied with my hand on the phone.

It was a hard enough course without the weather. Some of the riders were wearing raincoats, a few were sitting on towels. There was one panel fence most of the horses were hitting, and another one right after a turn seemed to confuse all of them.

I picked up the phone.

"Don't call," Jules said.

Ignoring the advice, I pressed the speed dial for Lockie.

"What? We're in the warm-up area."

Now there was both thunder and lightning at the showgrounds.

"Tell her to scratch if she doesn't feel confident. The weather looks terrible. The sportscaster said riders have been scratching already."

"Thanks for letting me know, Tal. I'll call you later."

"Tell me you put studs in his shoes."

"Yes. I'm not a beginner at this."

"I am."

Never using studs until Lockie came to the farm, there was no need for them since I had made it a policy to never show in the rain. It was bad enough to be at a show, why should I be cold and wet, too.

"She'll be fine. Let her do this," Lockie said. "Put Joly in your lap and I'll call you later. Bye."

He hung up.

"Joly?" I said into the air.

A moment later, from some other room in the house, the puppy found his way to my chair and I picked him up.

"How did you train him to do that," Cap asked.

"We didn't. He wants to be with us," I replied with my eyes on the monitor.

The rain was pooling in the low areas of the ring and horses were splashing as they galloped for the fences.

I hugged Joly.

"What's the worst that can happen," Cap asked.

She hadn't been given the details of Lockie's accident which had happened in the rain and mud. He was very lucky to have survived being thrown into the jump after Wingspread refused it.

I was sure Wing hadn't believed he could negotiate the berm. Maybe there would have been a rotational fall and one or both of them injured severely or even worse. I believed in the wisdom of the horse but Wing couldn't predict the outcome of his stop and I could.

"Don't buy trouble, Talia," Jules said as she put her hand on my arm. "No one's had any problems."

"With each horse, the footing deteriorates," I replied.

Cap studied the screen. "The ground doesn't seem that bad. Seriously."

I looked closer. All I could see was splashing water as the horse in the ring hit the top rail of a three stride to a three stride.

"The riders need goggles with little windshield wipers on them," Jules said trying to lighten the mood.

The horse and rider completed the course over the time and with either faults. Greer and Counterpoint entered the ring.

It was as if a fire hose had been turned on from above as she took her time to make a large circle, showing Counterpoint the fences. That was provided he could see them at all through the sheets of water coming down on them.

As Greer headed for the first fence, a plain vertical to get everyone into the spirit of the thing, I was silently begging her not to take any chances—just make it out in one piece. Counterpoint jumped clear and they went on to the next fence, an oxer with enormous bright orange oranges as the wings.

They made the right hand turn for the fences near the track, then cut through the diagonal to take the narrow fence and the alligator, the official state reptile of Florida. I was sure Teche would approve of that most delicious of creatures, so he claimed, being featured in the competition.

I was holding my breath as Greer turned for the panel fence that was giving so many horses trouble. They cleared it easily and made the rather tight turn for the final two jumps. With no faults, she had come in fourth.

"If she had jumped before it started to rain," Cap started, "she would have had a better time."

I was so glad she hadn't pushed for speed under the terrible conditions that now existed.

My phone started to ring and I clicked it on.

"You can start breathing again, Silly," Lockie said.

∽ 5 ∾

THE MOMENT Bijou stepped off the trailer a few days later, I knew why Cap never wanted to part with him. He was cute and had a kind eye. Maybe the gelding wasn't destined for gold medals but he was sure to win the heart of anyone who met him and was the first permanent resident in the new barn.

Cap and I had talked about whether the sales horses should be in the new barn or if it was better to have them in the original building. We decided that in the middle of the winter it didn't make any difference.

When Poppy and Gincy came for their lesson, the pleading began. It would be so much easier for them if their ponies lived at Bittersweet Farm was the argument.

I had no counterargument because it was still Lockie's decision to make. Were we going to be a boarding barn? I had no idea. It was true that many top coaches had their riders board at their stables, but that wasn't the situation at Bittersweet. Poppy and Gincy had been accepted as students to help them out but didn't know how long that would be. How many sales horses Lockie would find once he returned from Florida was impossible to predict. My sense was that he wanted to fill the stalls in the new barn with transient horses while the older barn would be for our horses and those in training.

In truth, part of it was the workload. Teche's help was temporary since he had so many horses in Florida. Once the winter show circuit was finished, those women would be needed at Acadiana Farm. We had Call and Cam's horse, Whiskey Tango laid up. We needed at least two more riders—Lockie and Greer—to exercise the horses in the barn now. Cap and I couldn't ride and do chores easily but had to.

I felt a bit sorry for her. Cap had no idea how much work there would be when she came east to help Lockie. She never complained and everything she did was perfect but if I was beginning to feel stressed out, there would come a time when Cap would, too. When CB nickered to me as I hurried down the aisle, I knew I wasn't taking the time for him that he deserved or that I wanted to spend with him. Often we'd come home from a hack after the sun had gone down and the snow creaked underneath his hooves.

***

Jules and I were watching Gourmet TV and I was about to give up in disgust when my phone rang. "Lockie," I said to Jules as I clicked it on.

"Isn't this the first time he called today?"

"They were traveling back to Napier," I said to her. "Hi."

"Hi, Silly. I saw the weather forecast for you and it looks as though the temperatures are going to drop tonight. Could you go over to the carriage house and check on the water? Let the kitchen faucet drip so the pipes don't freeze and burst."

"Didn't we drain them?"

"No, I don't remember that we did."

I thought we had. "Okay. I'll go check and have Pavel take care of it tomorrow if we forgot."

"Thanks. Call me when you're done and I'll tell you what Cam did today. Is this when I say bye?"

"You don't have to ask. You can just imagine at the end of the conversation, that's the right time," I replied.

"This seems to be the end, so bye until later."

"Bye, Lockie."

I clicked off, shook my head and stood. "I have to go check the pipes at the carriage house, I'll be back in a couple minutes. Maybe this show about squid will be over by then."

"The next one is about langoustines and how they can be used in dessert preparations."

"I'd rather go to bed," I replied leaving the room.

A couple minutes later, I stopped my truck in front of the carriage house and the security lights came on. It was cold but I still had a vague memory of taking care of the pipes but that might have been in December so it was right to check.

I opened the door, and noticed the change in temperature as I flipped the lights on by the door.

"Hi, Tal."

I stepped closer and put my arms around him. "That's a long way to travel to check your pipes."

Lockie held me tight. "You know I didn't come for the plumbing."

My face was pressed against his shoulder. "Why did you fly fifteen hundred miles?"

"I missed you. I told everyone I had to finalize the deal for Sora."

"Which part of that is true?"

"Both."

The fire was just beginning to catch on in the fireplace and he had turned the furnace on.

"Did you eat?" I asked.

"Chartier Foods is bringing out a line of microwave meals, so everyone on the flight had one of those."

"How was it?"

"He may have been born in the backcountry but he has multiple business degrees. Everything Teche touches turns to gold and this Cajun Chow is not going to be any different. Very tasty."

"Is he planning a chain of fast food restaurants?"

Lockie laughed. "Not that he's announced to me. He's been going to Vegas."

"Maybe he's going to come up with a Swamp Casino," I said. "Spanish moss will be dripping from the ceilings, he'll have Zydeco bands playing 24/7."

"One of the restaurants could be a riverboat theme," Lockie said as he placed another log on the fire now that the kindling had caught on.

"One could be The House of the Rising Sun," I replied, then sang the folksong.

"There is a house
"In New Orleans
"You call the Rising Sun
"It's been the ruin of many a poor soul
"And me, oh god, I'm one.
"If I'd listened what mama said
"I'd be at home today
"Being so young and foolish, poor girl
"Let a gambler lead me astray."

Lockie looked up. "What? It's about a girl?"

"Yes."

"No. It's about a guy who visits the working girls and then can't give up the debased lifestyle."

"It's about a working girl with a mean boyfriend."

Lockie shook his head. "That would be a given. Your argument sounds convincing but—"

"You don't believe me."

"I don't disbelieve you..." Lockie finished tinkering with the fire and came over to sit next to me on the sofa. "I've only heard it performed by men."

"I understand. People are convinced they know something and it turns out they don't. It's a big shock."

"I know I'm glad to be home," Lockie said. "Tell me the truth. How are you and Cap managing?"

"Some days are better than others."

"When it's cold, everything becomes more difficult."

"Yes."

"Sora is leaving in a few days. Thanks for helping me get her sold."

"Bijou arrived from California today."

"Cap's horse."

I nodded.

"Let me think about it and redo the schedule."

"I'm sorry. I feel as though I should be more competent at this."

Lockie put his arm around me. "There are horses laid up, many in training and you really don't have enough help for chores. We'll figure it out. I'd say I could find someone but—"

"Everyone's in Florida. Pavel's trying."

Helping at the barn was not Pavel's job. He was the groundskeeper. That meant he had always taken care of the house, the fences, the trees, the hay and everything else about the farm. All his other duties hadn't stopped because I needed help in the barn. Yes, we had Tomasz but he was helping Pavel who had trouble with his knees and was finding it progressively more difficult to do all he once did.

It was difficult to replace Lockie at the barn. His work ethic was superior and sometimes to his detriment. He didn't know when he'd had enough. On the other hand, I knew well in advance of when I had.

I turned off the light and the only illumination was from the fire.

"How is Greer doing?"

"Very impressive. Her ride in the downpour was skillful to say the least, but people have been coming up to me to comment on her ability. It's a little hard to believe but she's a very quiet rider."

Out of necessity, over the years Greer had learned how to turn inward, centering herself, making the best of a bad situation. When she didn't control her energy, Greer could be a human tempest.

"I'm not surprised. You must be pleased."

"For us both. Every positive experience increases her confidence."

"And Counterpoint?"

"He's a good horse for her. He's got the scope to jump her out of situations a more experienced rider would have avoided. Greer has the composure to make it look good no matter what's going on."

"She's not disappointed that they haven't won a class?"

"That doesn't seem to be the case. If everything is treated as training with no expectations, there's not much pressure. She doesn't know anyone she's competing against, and I think that helps. Nicole Boisvert is not bringing home the silver trophies the way she did as a junior which is obvious to everyone on the circuit. And Victoria went to England on an antiques buying trip so she's not standing around making Greer feel like she could have done better."

Greer hadn't mentioned that her mother had left Florida but most of our conversations were about important considerations like the Ambassador of Good Cheer project and how our second team was coming along.

"Now that the small talk is out of the way," Lockie started. "How are you doing?"

My throat tightened, words could not come out and I brought my fist down on my thigh.

"Talia?"

I shook my head in frustration.

"I know."

***

I stayed awake as long as possible to feel him beside me then the next thing I knew his phone woke us.

Lockie listened, then put it back on the nightstand. "The jet leaves at noon. Teche has a fundraiser to attend this evening."

"Is this his normal life?" I snugged myself closer to him.

"It seems to be. I've never met anyone with more energy. Silly, we have to get up."

"Lockie."

"I know, but I have to check on the horses, see Sora, and see your father." He pushed back the covers. "Is there anything you need to tell me?"

"Don't go back to Florida."

Lockie laughed. "About the barn."

"Poppy and Gincy want to board their ponies here."

He pulled on his jeans. "And the problem with that is..."

"It's your operation."

"You're co-manager," he said as he pulled on his shirt.

I sat up. "That's nice of you to say but it's not true and I don't want it to be true."

"You have three students."

"By accident." I reluctantly left the warm bed and cottony soft sheets. "I'm just trying to drag it all to the point where you're home and it can be dumped at your doorstep again."

"That's a goal. What's your objection to having the ponies here?"

"It's more work for starters and if the girls are comfortable here, they won't look for a new trainer. That's was the deal. I said I would do it on a temporary basis."

"All right. Does this work for you? I'll find someone to help with the chores. You take the ponies on for the winter and I'll find them a trainer in the spring."

I wasn't getting out of it. "Okay."

***

"I made all your favorites," Jules told Lockie with a huge hug as we came in the kitchen from the barn.

"You spoil me," he replied.

"Do I? Then I'll stop." Her smile illuminated the kitchen more than the track lighting over the butcher block work area.

"Is Andrew up and about yet?" Lockie asked.

My father entered the kitchen in casual clothes, which meant he was staying home for the day. I was always glad about that now.

"I am. Let's go to the den and you can tell me how things are going at Bittersweet South."

50

They left the kitchen together and I felt the familiar tug of increased distance.

Jules reached out and rubbed my shoulder. "How are you doing?"

I had to take a deep breath. "I'm better when he's here."

"I know."

I leaned against the countertop. "He'll always be traveling. There will always be a show to attend or horses to buy and sell."

"Your father doesn't stay home."

I nodded. "I didn't care until recently."

Jules finished sautéing the mushrooms in the pan then poured beaten eggs over them. "The last months have been a big change for you and Greer."

"After my mother passed, I only felt anger. That didn't hurt."

Jules grated cheese over the eggs. "You're not fully alive if you don't feel pain."

"If you can't feel pain, you can't feel real joy."

"That's right. Did your mother say that?"

"Yes."

"So does mine." Jules lifted the edge of the omelet, letting the custard flood underneath. "I know right now you don't believe this, but there is something beneficial to a relationship to be separated."

"Correct. I don't believe it."

"You appreciate each other more."

"Or you forget about each other."

Jules made a face at me then transferred the omelet to a plate. "Maybe there wasn't much of substance to begin with, in that case."

"I don't know the answer to that," I admitted.

Everything I had seen in my early life had been overly dramatic, fraught with life and death issues, hysteria, petulant demands, and silence. Maybe I couldn't understand the mechanism.

"You do," Jules assured me.

"That guy you were dating..." I started.

"The vegetarian?"

"Yeah. What made that relationship fail? I always thought it was because you moved here to the farm."

"That's true."

"Proves my point," I replied, taking the croissants out of the oven. "He's in Westchester barely two hours away and—kaput!"

Jules laughed. "No. I like you better than I liked him. The distance and our work had nothing to do with it."

Lockie and my father entered the kitchen, smiling. "Greer's happy. I'm happy. A horse was sold so the accountant is happy. Let's eat."

The door opened and Cap came in. "Is your phone turned off, Tal?"

"Yes."

Lockie gave me a look.

"I didn't want to be interrupted."

"The Waynes texted me when they couldn't get a hold of you. The Ponytude video is live on viewtube."

"Let's see it," my father said.

My laptop was where I had left it yesterday on the Hoosier cabinet so I picked it up, placed it on the kitchen table, and turned it on. A moment later, I found the account the Waynes had created for the farm, and clicked on *How Your Pony Doesn't Lead You*.

I was astonished by the professionalism that went into the video. It was indistinguishable from a very short movie, with titles, in-focus camera work and excellent sound even though the wind had been blowing that afternoon.

We got to the part where Jos was skiing behind Foxy, and felt like digging a hole for myself. Poor kid. I asked the Waynes not to use that part but there it was and from two different camera angles. Then I realized everyone around the table was laughing.

Jules put her arm around me and gave me a big squeeze.

"Very well done, Talia," my father said as he pulled Jules's chair out for her.

"Are all the instructional videos going to be funny like that?" Jules asked.

I sat down. "All? This is it. There are no more."

Lockie sat next to me and winked.

***

We had just enough time to tack CB and Wing and go on a short hack, so we walked them to the stream. The banks and rocks were slick with ice and we kept back.

"I won't miss this weather," Lockie said as we headed for home. "It's very agreeable in Florida right now."

I didn't know what to say. Of course I wanted him to be comfortable and of course I wanted him to do what he loved to do. And of course I wished the situation was different. I had quite a lot of experience with wishing things were not as they were and knowing they weren't going to change.

"Come down for a weekend," Lockie said. "We'll find someone to replace you here for three days."

"Tempting," I replied, although it wasn't really.

Besides the very agreeable weather, it sounded like everything I didn't like about horse shows. There were a large number of owners, riders and grooms for a large number of horses all swirling through a party atmosphere. Greer had always enjoyed the socializing but I never had.

The best show I had attended was the one in the autumn when Lockie rode CB in a dressage class. I acted as the groom. We stayed for the one class and came home. Hanging out all day, listening to gossip about people I didn't know, was not my idea of a good time.

"Would you come down to Florida because I miss you?"
He held out his hand to me.

I took it. "Of course."

6

LOCKIE LEFT BEFORE LUNCH. The afternoon was filled with exercising horses and chores. I called the Becks and told them they could board Tango Pirate at Bittersweet for the winter. Then I called the Hambletts and gave them the news for Gincy and Beau Peep. They were so happy, the cost of board and lessons didn't make an impression.

Cap and I had researched the prices for similar situations in the Northeast. I wouldn't charge for lessons the way proven trainers did, but it was not an inexpensive choice. The girls would be on a schedule of three lessons a week and could come every day to ride their ponies, if they wanted to. I hoped the Hambletts and the Becks could share the chauffeuring duties, otherwise both families were going to do a great deal of driving.

From the feed store, I picked up a notice of local indoor shows being held in the next months. One a month seemed sufficient as feedback for how their training was progressing.

If the girls wanted to show every weekend, I had no objection, but wasn't going to attend with them. It wasn't realistic to think three lessons were enough to cause significant improvement in their riding. If it was for fun, that was fine. Both Gincy and Poppy had more than enough stage presence for their age. They weren't nervous about showing so there was very little to be gained by showing three weekends a month in the middle of winter. The most they'd get was a ribbon and frostbite from standing outside waiting to go into the indoor for a class.

I hoped to increase their dressage skills and thought a show in March would be a good test of their progress. With their pony hunters, neither girl had much experience with dressage but that training would improve them more as riders than yet another pony hunter over fences class would.

It all depended on what results we wanted. I wanted better riders and well-schooled ponies. If it was about ribbons and trophies and making it to the pony hunter finals at Harrisburg, then I was really going to be wasting their time.

My phone rang and I barely got hello out when Greer started.

"He is so rude!"

"Who?"

"Cam!"

"What did he do?"

"He kept me waiting for fifteen minutes today."

Back to the atomic clock. One of us should have warned Cam how being off her schedule sent Greer into a paroxysm of indignation.

"Did he apologize?"

"He brushed it off!"

"Maybe it was something important," I suggested.

"Sloane Radclyffe!"

"Who's that?" Not only did I not pay attention to who these people were, I made a concerted effort not to know.

"Tch!"

Greer was more upset than she had been in weeks.

"The Scintillating Socialite trademark pending."

I still had never heard of her.

"Her great-greatgrandfather was called the Python of Pennsylvania Petroleum."

"There's oil in Pennsylvania?" I asked. "I'm sorry. I'm not up on the geology of all fifty states."

"They're floating on oil and natural gas," Greer replied.

"I didn't know."

"Totally new money," Greer practically spit.

It didn't sound so new to me but I refrained from commenting on the longevity of their fortune.

"He was friends with all the famous robber barons—Carnegie, Mellon, Flagler."

"So this person is in Florida? Does she have horses?"

"They have a huge farm in Southern Pennsylvania, outside of Philadelphia. She brought a couple of her nags to Florida. Haven't you ever heard of Midnite Socialite?"

"No."

"Open jumper."

"Oh."

"Black. Not a white hair on him."

It was starting to occur to me that this wasn't about fifteen minutes, it was about this chick. Why, though? Greer had never expressed any interest in Cam besides as a trainer and barely about that.

"Avoid her," I said.

"She's followed by photographers and reporters getting in everyone's way," Greer replied.

"Why?"

"She's the Scintillating Socialite!"

"This is important to people?" I was completely confused since I had never been a fan if any so-called celebrity.

"Yes."

"Well, you're minor royalty, so I think that trumps being a socialite."

"Not hardly."

"Is their house bigger than your grandparents' house"

"You mean the country house that is open to tourists parading through because the Kensington-Rowes can't afford the taxes and upkeep?"

I had seen a photo of the Kensington-Rowe house years ago, but thought Greer was yanking my lead shank by showing me a building big enough to be a city's public library.

"No lookie-loos come through the Swope house and you don't have photographers trying to catch you in the middle of an indiscretion, so you're better off than the socialite."

There was silence.

"Yeah," Greer said softly. "Okay. I have to go. I'll call you later."

She disappeared before I could say goodbye.

I hadn't found the right things to say because I didn't understand the generation of her distress. With Greer it could be anything. It could seem to be one thing and wind up being something else. It could be the horse. It could be something that happened when she lived in England that I didn't know about.

Or it could be that she thought Cam was her trainer exclusively.

***

By the time I got into bed, Greer had sent me a list of articles that appeared on the Internet featuring the Scintillating Socialite. Sloane Radclyffe did live on an estate, in a three-story house on a river where students rowed sculls and she gave dinner parties at the water's edge. She was small, slight and not particularly lovely but that didn't seem to hamper her social life. From all reports, her dance card was filled by several attractive young bachelors who were photographed with her at a variety of society events.

Huge sums of money can be a huge aphrodisiac. It's something like drinking in a bar. The later it gets, the better the people look.

My mother told me that in the last months of her life as she tried to provide all the advice I might need in the future when she wasn't there to guide me. She shouldn't have worried so much. My grandparents stepped right up and came as close as I would let them. It was a difficult time for me and everyone was probably too deferential, except Greer. I wouldn't have had that much patience with me as the adults had.

The phone rang.

"Who could that be, Joly?"

The puppy was sound asleep next to me and didn't wake.

I clicked on the phone. "Hello," I said.

"Hi."

"Who's this?"

"You know who it is."

"Are you the guy who is in and out of my life like the wooden bird in a cuckoo clock?"

"Have you been hitting Jules's cooking sherry?"

"Should I?"

"No," Lockie replied.

"Maybe I should be hitting CB's stash of stout."

"No."

I paused for a long moment, snapping my fingers. "You're the blue-eyed guy, right?"

"That's me."

"Are you the cute one?"

"If you don't remember me, I'll go back to the pool party."

"Mean!"

"What?"

"I'm in flannel PJs freezing my butt off, with only a small puppy to keep me warm and you're trying to make me jealous by conjuring images of model-thin girls in tiny bikinis."

"Did it work?" Lockie asked.

"Sorry. No."

"Last time I looked, you were model thin."

"Are you looking at me?" I asked.

"I'd be a fool not to." He paused. "Talia, there's something I didn't tell you while I was up there. That video you did was very sweet. You're doing fine without me."

He was just seeing the façade. Yes, the stalls were clean and the aisle was swept, but, day by day, I wasn't keeping up. "I'm not! I'm losing my design margin!"

"Excuse me?"

"The capacity of a system beyond its expected load."

At some point, I couldn't juggle hard enough or fast enough to do everything that needed to be done.

"I should be auditing your classes with Amanda. This is way beyond me."

I took a deep breath. "Come home, Lockie."

He laughed. "I just got here."

"It seems longer than that."

***

My morning seemed extra busy with the farrier and vet coming to check Call's wound. Fortunately, all was well and the pony was permitted more freedom. We had been more upset by his confinement in the stall than he had been but I fully expected him to attempt a couple wild bucks the first time he was ridden.

Before noon, I drove to the feed store to pick up a couple items while Cap began bringing horses in who had

63

been turned out earlier. We were sticking to the schedule. Just barely. Later in the afternoon, I had the pony riders coming for a lesson, and a friend of a friend of Cap's who might be able to help us out.

I hurried into the house, late for lunch because Mr. Orlek, owner of the feed store, was talkative. It was hard to blame him. In the middle of the winter, there weren't many customers for gardening products or flats of flowers.

"Rosemary Booth called while you were out," Cap said.

I hung my jacket on a peg and picked up Joly who had come to greet me. "How is she?"

"She asked if we can keep her horse here for a while."

"Is she all right?"

"She said she was going to New Zealand and Micronesia."

"Nice!"

Tyr was a warmblood with a sweet personality that she had bought from us some months back. He had seen her in good stead on the hunt field but now the season was over so maybe life had become too predictable.

One more horse to exercise, but at least we had the extra stall for him.

"I guess the answer is yes. You'll like him, Cap."

She laughed. "My knee patches are falling off my breeches already."

Jules put beef and barley soup in front of us. "Talia sent for the cutest breeches last year, and wisely bought them on sale."

Lockie didn't agree that it was so wise because he watched every expenditure like a hawk and thought it was a splurge we didn't need, but still the rest of us were happy with them.

"I have a few pairs that will fit you if you don't mind fun colors," I replied, putting Joly on the floor.

Cap reached for a roll. "What do you consider fun?"

"They're in the colors of sherbet. Yellow. Ocean blue. Celery. Melon."

Cap nodded. "Yeah. Fun."

***

I trimmed CB's whiskers, neatened up his mane a little, snuggled then dressed him for an arctic exploration of the pasture. Cap and I made arrangements to go pick up Tyr from Rosemary's barn before the pony riders arrived then I went up to the house to get some hot tea for the trip.

As I was waiting for the water to heat, my phone rang.

"Greer had a class this morning," I told Jules.

"Why didn't we watch?"

"They're not streaming every class, just the big ones." I clicked on the phone. "Hi."

"You will never believe who came up to me after the class," Greer said.

"Do you really want me to try to guess or will you tell me?"

"George Morris."

The last word on equitation and hunters, he had ridden in the Rome Olympics and was the youngest rider in history to win the Medal and the Maclay. "Wow. Wait. What did he say?"

"He congratulated me saying I was one of the few younger competitors who rides in the classical style. Then he complimented my trainer and asked who it was. I said Lockie Malone."

"Then what happened," I asked.

"He smiled and walked away."

"Tell Lockie."

"I haven't seen him since. He went with Teche to look at horses."

Lockie had to be so happy in Florida. So much of his life had been doing exactly what he was doing now. Then to have George Morris compliment his student, that was just about as good as things could get. Giving up eventing had to be difficult, but maybe this was the beginning of compensation.

Jules gave me the market basket with the tea and some noshes and I got in Lockie's truck. There was no point to take the van just to go locally for one horse.

We arrived at Rosemary's house, and Tyr was waiting for us, blanketed and wrapped for his journey. He walked into the trailer without hesitation and, hoping he wasn't worried about where he was going, I reassured him that he would recognize Bittersweet when he got there. He would be in the new barn, but I would put Butch in the stall next to him so Tyr would know someone.

By the time we got back, Poppy and Gincy had arrived. The ponies were tacked, and warmed up in the indoor ring as I entered. We worked on the flat, a good deal of the time without stirrups, going over the basics as I tried to convince them that any aid they used whether hands, legs or seat should be quiet not loud. They needed to learn how to recalibrate everything they did, refine all their movements so that were in harmony with their ponies. I wanted to get them confirmed in the mindset of being a better rider for real in their pony's estimation rather than a horse show judge. That was the only opinion that really mattered.

Cap took over as the session was finished, explaining to Poppy and Gincy what would be expected of them here at Bittersweet, and safety would always be the first consideration. I left as they went to the new barn as though they thought it was Versailles Palace.

The moment I stepped through the kitchen door, Jules looked up from preparing dinner and said "Call Greer."

I could tell something was amiss but had no idea what. I hoped it was that Cam was late for her afternoon class. "Why didn't she call me?"

"I have no idea but she's upset."

"On a scale of one to ten, how upset?"

"Twenty."

My phone rang.

"That must be her." I looked at it. Lockie. I clicked it on. "Hi."

"Did Greer talk to you this afternoon?"

"No, but she spoke to Jules. What happened?"

"She had an ami-owner class and did well. Counterpoint hit the white top rail just like most of the horses did."

"So she had some kind of confrontation with Cam?"

Cam had blamed a white top rail for Whiskey's leg injury but Greer never believed it.

"No. Yes. But when she returned to the stabling area, she saw Nanci Huet whaling away on her horse for hitting the same fence in the open jumping class."

"Nanci Huet is one of the top riders in the country. Why would she hit her horse?"

"Because of $25,000 in prize money could be the explanation."

My heart sank. "Then what happened?"

"Greer used her phone to record this incident and called the police, charging animal abuse. She's at the police station now giving a statement."

"Why aren't you there with her?"

"Don't start, Talia. Counterpoint hit his shin pretty hard, so I spent the afternoon with the vet. Cam is with her."

"I'm sorry. It's just very upsetting."

"This woman is an icon with a sterling reputation and it was destroyed by someone no one had ever heard of at lunchtime. Everyone on the show grounds is shaken. You can't tell me anything I don't know."

"Are you angry with her?"

"I wish she had come to me before calling the police."

"Why? Would you have covered up for this Huet bitch?"

The connection went dead.

I dropped the phone on the counter. "Joly. Let's go for a walk."

The puppy ran up to me and we made three laps around the pond before I was able to go back inside.

***

By the time I entered the house, my father knew. The Springston police had called to assure him that his daughter did not need a lawyer.

That was a relief.

I removed my jacket and hung it up by the door.

"Talia," Jules began. "Call Lockie."

"Did he call?"

"No. Apologize."

I reached for a cherry tomato in the salad bowl and ate it.

"I love you. I love Lockie. What would your mother tell you to do?"

"Be a big picture person."

"Decide what's important to you and act on it," Jules replied.

"I don't even know what happened."

"Why is that important?" Jules asked.

Joly came over and sat on my foot. I shook my head. "It's not."

"We'll wait dinner for you." Jules turned off the pot of water simmering on the stove.

Gathering Joly into my arms, we went upstairs and I put him on my bed. "If you're really good, and Lockie doesn't hang up on me again, I'll put you on the phone."

Joly tilted his head.

"No promises, though."

He wagged his tail.

I keyed in Lockie's cell phone.

"What?"

"I'm calling to apologize. I'm sorry, so be nice about it."

"I'm standing in a wash stall with Counterpoint wearing ice boots. I haven't eaten since last night and my head feels like it's going to split open."

"So two years after the accident, the pain finally catches up with you."

"Something like that."

"Your pills are in your room?"

"Yes."

"Is it foolish for me to suggest you carry a little pillbox with you?"

"No, it's a good idea. Where do you get them?"

"I'll send one to you."

"I'm sorry I hung up. I was angry that you thought I would defend Nanci Huet abusing her horse."

"That's not what I meant. I wasn't thinking but knowing you..."

"What."

"I didn't want you to let her off the hook, to protect her reputation, or to make it possible for her to avoid taking responsibility for her actions at your expense."

"How would it be at my expense?"

"You haven't eaten, you're obviously alone with Counterpoint, you have a headache. No one is taking care of you, including you, and your instinct is to make things easy for everyone else."

"It's just one day. One lousy day."

I put my hand on Joly's soft coat. "Can we try to solve your situation right now? When can you eat? When can you call the day over?"

"I don't know."

"Where's Tracy? Can she finish up with Counterpoint?"

"She doesn't have the experience. Don't worry about it."

How was it possible for me to not worry? "All right. Try to call me when you get back to your room so I know you're okay."

"That's it?"

"Yes. You said you're fine. I have to believe you."

"I'll call you later then."

"Great. Bye."

"Bye."

The moment he hung up, I called Teche's house phone and made arrangements for dinner to be brought to his room. Then I called Tracy and told her to drop what she was doing and go help Lockie without telling him I insisted upon it.

Before I put down the phone, Greer called.

"I'm a pariah," she said.

That was probably an understatement. "Where are you?"

"Back at Acadiana South."

"Where's Cam?"

"Here."

"Tell him to go to the barn and help Lockie."

"Why does Lockie need help?"

"Because your horse is lame."

"I didn't know we hit the rail that hard," Greer replied. "I'll go." She was silent for a moment. "He has a headache?"

"Yes."

"I'll make sure he gets back to his room."

"And that he eats. I called the house and they're making him something for dinner."

"Okay, Tal. Don't lose it. I'll make sure he eats and goes to bed."

"Thank you."

"No one thinks so here, but I did the right thing."

I held Joly up to the phone then put him back on the bed. "That was Joly. He says he knows you did."

∽ 7 ∾

INSTEAD OF GETTING BETTER, things got worse.

The images of Nanci Huet weren't on the Internet because the police confiscated Greer's phone, but the story was on Twitter and Facebook and every horse site that existed. This was a big damn deal.

About half the opinion ran against Greer with the feeling she should have perhaps interrupted the whipping and Nanci would have been ashamed enough to stop.

I thought that was unrealistic at best. She would have stopped and been more circumspect the next time, if she was able to control her temper.

The other half of the opinion was of the delight and glee as is exhibited when any celebrity fails in public. Some of these people took Greer's side but most didn't know her name. Very few people knew who she was. She hadn't won in class in Florida and there was gossip that she was simply a spoiled brat whose father had bought her an expensive horse she wasn't good enough to ride to first place. It had to be hell for Greer.

I went down to the barn early and once the horses were fed, picked out CB's stall, then sat on a flake of hay while he ate around me. After explaining everything that happened in Florida, I stopped. "I had an idea. It would be nice if you cooperated but if you object, I'll think of something else."

He nuzzled my jacket looking for a carrot.

"Am I just like one big vending machine to you?"

CB pushed his nose into my face and slimed me with hay spit, so I pulled a piece of carrot out of my pocket and offered it to him.

I couldn't bear to think of what kind of life Nanci Huet's horse had. The only positive thought I could conjure was that his grooms probably showed him some affection and respect.

My phone rang and I managed to find it.

"Hi. Are you okay?"

"They're not running me out of town, yet," Greer said.

"I'm so sorry."

"Don't be sorry for me."

"All right."

"Dad called. He said he was never more proud of me."

I reached out to touch CB's ankle to let him know I was still there and moved my leg so he wouldn't step on me. "That's very sad, in one respect."

"How so?" Greer asked.

"You're one hundred percent Swope now. You couldn't go back to the Rowe side of your family even if you wanted to."

"I don't want to."

I stood so CB could have access to the rest of his hay. "Have you seen Lockie? He didn't call me last night."

"Not this morning. Last night I stayed with him and made sure he ate. Lockie took his pills and they knocked him right out. He didn't even take a shower, just lay down on the bed and that was it."

"Did you check on him this morning?" I asked.

"Let me ask you a question, Tal. Were you always worried that your mother was going to die overnight when you weren't standing watch?"

I took a deep breath. "Yes."

"Lockie's not going to die. Take a break for a change. We'll all be happier for it."

***

I exercised Wing and Citabria, then went up to the house for lunch. It smelled wonderful in the kitchen.

Joly ran up to greet me and as soon as I hung up my jacket, I picked him up for a hug.

"What are you making?"

Jules smiled. "I'm inventing. These are Giddyup-and-Goes." She pointed to a rack full of beautiful chocolate cupcakes topped with a swirl of pink buttercream frosting flecked with red bits. The cupcake liners were a pink polka dot design.

"What's the red?"

"Diced cherries. Each cupcake has a griottine cherry inside sitting in a puddle of kirsch ganache."

I reached for one.

Jules waved a wooden spoon at me. "They are for later."

"What's happening later?"

"When the manure hits the fan."

"I'm not up to speed."

"The phone's been ringing all morning. Equine reporters have sensed the story and have their noses in the dirt trying to track Miss Swope down."

"What did you say?"

"*Non parlo Inglese. Chiama più tardi.*" Jules laughed. "That's what we always say at my family's house when the vultures call."

"We have an unlisted number."

"Someone ratted you out," Jules replied as she finished decorating the last cupcake.

There were so many people who had a number to Bittersweet Farm at this point that it wasn't a surprise a journalist would be able find us. Greer was riding for the farm, the name was on the tack trunks. No one needed to be an ace detective to figure this non-mystery out.

"As long as they don't link Greer to her mother and that horrible book."

"You mean the book that's now number one?"

I hugged Joly closer. "Is it?"

"Yes."

Tight Chaps and Loose Tarts. We all thought it would be out of our lives by now. Maybe in a way it was never in our lives but I believed Greer's mother, Victoria, had modeled the love interest after Cam. I didn't know who the female lead was. Victoria herself, probably. As long as this nutty piece of erotica was selling on the Internet, it was in our lives and consciousness.

I had no idea how we had gone from a backwater, country horse farm, to having ties to a sex book and now every equestrian journalist in the country trying to get a story out of Greer. She had seen a crime being committed, and phoned the police. It was so simple. It was the kind of incident that happened every day, but because it centered around this well-known Huet woman, beloved by all, except apparently by her horses, then it was a hot news item.

The house phone rang.

"Don't answer it," Jules said.

"Now we have to pretend we're not home," I replied as Joly and I headed toward my father's den.

The door was open so I entered. "Hi. Lunch is ready."

He put the cap on his fountain pen and placed it on the desk. "Are you worried about Greer?"

"Yes."

"What would you like to do?"

"Bring her home."

"She needs to make that decision for herself."

I nodded. "She may not be thinking clearly."

"We had a long talk. I thought she was making sense. Greer did the right thing and she's standing her ground even though there are those on the show circuit who believe she shouldn't have taken the incident public."

"You don't know everything about her."

"No, I'm sure I don't," my father admitted. "If she wanted me to know, she'd tell me." He stood. "You have to give people a chance, Tal."

I shook my head.

"This is home. It's not a walled sanctuary. Being here is not going to protect any of us from the outside world."

"She would be with us!"

"She's got Lockie and Cam and Tracy."

We walked into the kitchen together and I put Joly on the floor.

My phone rang, I checked it and clicked it on.

"You're not answering the phone at the house?"

"No, was that you?"

"Yes, I thought you would be in for lunch," Lockie said.

"We are. I wish you were here."

"That would be nice. I just got a call from one of the grooms at the Huet stable. That horse of hers is very lame. They're in crisis mode with three different veterinarians on site."

"Do they know what the problem is?"

"If it was something obvious, I would have been told."

"This situation is just getting worse."

"Prepare yourself," Lockie said.

***

By the time I got into bed, the news of Diamantin was on the Internet. The horse had been taken from the stable to a high tech veterinary hospital where they would use the same kind of medical devices used on humans on the gelding to determine why he was lame.

Shutting off my laptop, I thought about going down to sit with CB for a while. As I pushed back the covers, my phone rang.

"Hi."

"Hi."

"Are you okay?" Lockie asked.

"If questioning everything is okay, then I'm fine."

"Silly. Listen to me."

"Are we going to have the same argument we always have?"

"Not as far as I'm concerned," Lockie said. "We'll start at the beginning. Horses are very delicate."

"You've just made my argument."

"If you don't want to ride, don't ride. You're not going to stop everyone else. Throughout history, horses have always worked. They still work. They don't pull plows or carriages, they become mounts for police, herd cattle, and even partner in sports events."

"And sport horses receive wonderful care, the finest hays and grains and people like me running around with a fork to pick up after them," I said, knowing the argument.

"Yes."

"And they're treated like Ferarris except that motor vehicles don't feel pain when you run them into a tree at a hundred and twenty miles an hour."

"Talia. You have a choice. Make it now. You can run Bittersweet Farm with the best interests of the horses in mind or you can quit."

"What kind of choice is that?"

"It's the choice you were taught by your mother. You care about everyone who comes into your life. You can stop doing that and the horses you could care for miss out, or you can accept that the world is not as you wish it, but go forward anyway."

"For the sake of the horses who come into our lives."

"Yes."

"Is it right to sell these horses?"

"Do you mean is it morally right?"

"Yes. You don't know where they will wind up."

"Talia. You don't know where I'll wind up. You couldn't hold onto your mother tightly enough. You have to be able to let go."

It took a long moment to get control of my voice. "Promise me, Lockie. Promise me that we will always try to find a good home for them."

"I promise you."

"Promise me you will never take any chances."

"I promise I will always wear my helmet."

He couldn't make a promise he knew he couldn't keep. I took a couple deep breaths. "That horse isn't going to recover, is he?"

"Miracles happen."

"So no."

"What did I just say? Miracles happen and accidents happen. I wasn't supposed to survive my accident but apparently there was more I had to do in my life. Holding your hand seems to be high on the list."

"Maybe it's part of your job specs," I replied.

"If it is, don't tell your father he doesn't have to pay me to do it."

"You'd do it for free?"

"For free? I'd pay him for the privilege."

"Lockie. Come home."

"As soon as I can. Tell me about the *Zuckerwuerfel*."

"The what?"

"Your pony riders. Sugar Cubes."

"They are pretty sweet," I replied. "I think I've lost Jos. She hasn't been here in days."

"There's an earthquake taking place in her family. Who are you going to get to ride Calling All Comets?"

"Poppy, for now."

"Think about letting Gincy ride him one day and Poppy ride him the next."

I knew that seemed to make sense but Call was smarter than Gincy. Beau was a little bit of a babysitter, taking care of her. Call needed someone who could think a stride ahead of him and Gincy wasn't at that point yet.

Neither was Jos but she had more determination, more stickiness. I would consider it a loss for all of us if Jos did give up riding. How she was going to solve her family problems was beyond me, and probably beyond her, too. It was obviously beyond her father who seemed to have given up somewhere along the way.

That was not in my father's personality. He wasn't capable of giving up. He wanted to be with my mother and if it had taken five years or ten, I don't think that would have made a difference. Fortunately or unfortunately, he didn't have to wait ten years. Once my mother became ill, in a way she deferred to his greater vitality and organizational capabilities. She let him take over when she couldn't go on. Maybe it was for me.

I thought Mr. Deering would be wise to consider Jos and what his attitude was doing to her life.

"I can't do anything about Jos," I said.

"No," Lockie agreed.

"Is that letting go?"

"Yes, Silly, it is."

***

I spent the next morning with CB, trimming his whiskers and his mane, singing him a song called *Run Away* after explaining he shouldn't take it literally. We rode in the indoor for twenty minutes, where he did his swish twice and then we went out for a hack as it was starting to snow.

After thanking him for the ride, I went up to the house.

"When is winter going to be over?" I asked Jules.

"It's not even February yet."

She started to make a grilled panini for me and I picked up Joly.

"Where is everyone?"

"If you mean your father, he went to the city to see your grandparents. Cap went to meet with someone who might want to help with the work and I'm going to make almond toffee cheesecake this afternoon. P.S. I wouldn't turn down help because I have to make the ricotta cheese first."

There was a knock at the kitchen door and Joly barked on cue.

I opened the door to Jos and a pretty woman with long hair and too much make-up for my tastes.

"Hi, Tal," Jos said.

"Come in out of the cold," I replied and closed the door as they entered.

"We can't stay but a minute," the woman said. "We're driving back to Nashville."

"The weather forecast is for snow," Jules replied.

"The farther south we go, the more the snow will become rain," the former Mrs. Deering explained.

Jos looked as though she was beyond tears. "Is it okay if I go to the barn and pick up my stuff?"

"Sure."

"We didn't want to sneak in and make it look like something it isn't. They're her things," the mother said as she put an arm around Jos's shoulders.

"Of course. Do you need any help, Jos?"

"No, thanks."

"We're fine," the mother said.

"Thanks for helping me with the riding," Jos managed to say as she was pulled to the door.

"It was a pleasure working with you," I replied.

"Bye."

I waved and the door closed.

Jules put my sandwich on a plate. "The mother's pretty but life will never be kind to her."

I put Joly on the floor and washed my hands. "Why not?"

We went to the table with our sandwiches and mugs of hot tea.

"I grew up in show business and have seen hundreds of people like her. They so desperately want to be famous. They have a little talent and they would step on anyone if it got them to the next level. She'll have a little success and that will be proof she's doing everything right. She'll do more of it."

I removed the tea bag from the mug. "I don't understand. People want to be famous, they want to succeed. Why is that bad?"

"If you want to sing, sing. If you want to ride, ride. If you want to cook, cook. That's your path. Where it leads you is a mystery, but you follow that path. You can't force it. Life doesn't like being coerced."

I took a bite of the grilled eggplant, sundried tomato and mozzarella panini. The olive oil had soaked into the thick bread and the press had melded all the flavors together into something greater than the sum of its parts.

"Think about Lockie's situation. Is he a good rider?"

"Wonderful."

"Why?" Jules asked.

I had no immediate answer. "He is built for it. He has the perfect body type and a natural elegance."

"That may be true, and I'm sure that helps but dig deeper, Talia."

I thought for a moment. "He loves to ride. He loves the horses, the work, the training, the smell of leather."

"This is what life rewards," Jules said.

"Some reward. Being thrown head first into a jump."

"That he survived and didn't complain, didn't blame anyone. He came here and under Greer's bad tempered assault in the early days, maintained his charming disposition, and eventually brought her around."

"And?"

"Lockie found a home where he's able to do exactly what he loves doing."

My fingers glistened from the olive oil squeezed from the sandwich and I wiped them on a napkin. "I'm glad he was able to go to Florida even though I miss him."

The highly competitive show circuit with the top riders and the best horses had been Lockie's world as a junior rider. He had shown equitation, hunters and jumpers at one time or another and knew everyone who was anyone. I knew he would have preferred eventing again, but was gracious enough to put that part of his life aside. That it was possible for Lockie to pick up close to where he left off was fortunate and I was pleased for him.

I still missed him.

My phone rang. "Joly. It's your mom. Would you like to speak to her?" I clicked the phone on and held it out for him but he was silent.

"Talia, are you there?" Greer said impatiently.

"Yes. I was letting Joly have a chance to say hi."

"Hi. Did you see the current issue of *Equestrian Culture*?"

"No."

"Did it come in the mail or not? You can look at it online if not."

I moved the phone from my ear. "Jules, did the mail come?"

She looked up at the ceiling.

"What now?" I asked.

"I hid it." Jules pointed to the drawer that caught all the odds and ends of our lives.

Getting up, I crossed the kitchen and pulled open the drawer to find the glossy magazine inside. Removing it, I glanced at the cover. "What?"

Jules shrugged.

"Do you see it?" Greer was back in her shriek mode.

I sat at the table and opened the magazine, found the page and read the headline. "*My Favorite Time of Day is Night.* Interview with Victoria Rowe author of the bestselling novel *Tight Chaps and Loose Tarts.*"

Greer was shrieking in Florida.

"Does she mention you?"

"No!"

"How did this happen?"

"How do I know? But I'm going to track that publisher down and give her hell."

"Is she in Florida?"

"Yes. She's everywhere, pushing free magazines into everyone's hands."

"I'm sorry."

"This interview with my mother, a little on the salacious side—"

"—Really?"

"Yes! Is bringing the magazine a ton of publicity here. And the editor gave that horrid book a great review. 'There aren't enough equestrian novels for adults'!"

I was trying to read the article and listen to Greer at the same time, but unfortunately had no talent for multitasking. It was my preference to do one thing then move onto the next.

"Promise me you won't run the editor over with the truck," I said.

"No, I'm not promising that."

Florida was falling apart for Greer and I didn't know how to help her.

8

"ARE YOU IN BED?" he asked.

"Yes. Reading. Trying to pretend I'm living in a dream world where I have one week of nothing bad happening."

"You mean Victoria," Lockie said.

"Greer is so upset."

"She is."

"Can you take her on a vacation?"

"Vacation?"

"Get her away for a couple days. Take her to..." I thought for a bit, "Ernest Hemingway's house in the Florida Keys. Amanda would approve."

"If you would like to fly down and take her to DisneyWorld, that's fine with me but I have horses to exercise for Teche. I can't leave now."

"I'm sorry. Of course you do. She's in so much pain. How did Greer wind up with a mother like that?"

"I don't know. What's the difference now? It's not a shock that Victoria wrote that stupid book."

"Maybe it was obscure before and easier to ignore. Now it's Number One. It's so...replete with descriptions that seem like personal experience."

"Greer's upset her mother had sex?"

"That kind of sex."

Lockie laughed. "You'll have to explain the different kinds of sex to me some day. I'll take notes."

"I'm not an authority on the topic," I replied.

"Greer—"

"Don't go there."

"No judgment."

"Greer made mistakes. That's another thing she finds quite upsetting and wants to put in the past but having her mother splash this...behavior so brazenly in public makes it very fresh in her mind."

There was a long pause. "You're both so complicated."

"Too complicated?"

"No, Silly."

"Let's change the topic. How is that horse?"

"Maybe it would be better if you didn't ask."

I stroked Joly's head. "So?"

"They think he ruptured a quadriceps and will be attempting to repair it tomorrow."

"Does Greer know?"

"Everyone knows. This is the big story of the WEF."

Winter Equestrian Festival.

I was beginning to think we would have been far better off having our own winter festival here at the farm. There could be a competition for skiing behind the horses. We could have found a sleigh for CB to pull across the frozen wastes of the pasture and I could have pretended to be a character in *Dr. Zhivago*. Lockie could have ridden Wing through the snowdrifts at sundown looking dramatic, handsome and Heathcliffish. He would have scored a perfect ten for that. That could have been our next and last video.

"Bigger than *Tight Chaps*?" I asked.

"Yes."

"I'll bet if everyone knew that Greer was Victoria's daughter, that would change things."

"Enough, Tal. Tell me about the horses."

"We lost Jos today. Her mother showed up to take her to Nashville."

"Could life be worse for her there than with her father?" Lockie asked.

It was a good question and I didn't have an answer. I was finding I had fewer answers than ever.

***

By nine the next morning the vet came to check Cam's horse, Whiskey Tango and his bruised coffin bone in order to determine if the gelding should continue to be hand-walked or if there was anything else we could do for him.

My phone began ringing as I walked Dr. Fortier out to his truck. "I have to get this," I said. "Thanks for the help with Whiskey."

"Have a good day, Talia. He'll be a hundred percent by spring."

I gave him a little wave and clicked on the phone.

"Hi, Greer."

"They're operating on that horse right now. There's a viewing area over the operating theater where it's possible to watch the surgery."

"How do you know that?"

"It's a famous facility. Everyone here knows of it."

"How is Counterpoint after he hit the rail?"

"He's fine. Lockie..." Greer paused then sighed. "I get why you like him."

I didn't know where she was going with this line of thought. "Okay."

"You deserve him. I don't..."

"Greer, please don't talk like that. Maybe it was true in the beginning that you were hard on him, but it hasn't been true for months. I'm not perfect. Very far from it. I say things the wrong way. I feel things the wrong way. We all miss the target. Lockie included."

"He must hate me."

"No, Lockie likes you and he said that to me a couple days ago. Put everything aside and concentrate on riding. That's what you're there to do. You had George Morris come up to you! You must be outstandingly good to have him notice you among all the hundreds of other riders there."

There was a long pause. "People only compliment me when they want something from me."

I would have held the phone to Joly's ear but he was in the house. "Joly holds you in the highest regard. You saved his life."

"It's a no-kill shelter so he was pretty safe."

"It's one thing to just be alive and it's another thing to experience compassion and affection the way he does now. You gave him that. Be proud of yourself."

"I couldn't help that horse," Greer said and hung up.

Sliding the phone back into my pocket, I returned to the barn where Pavel and Tomasz were repairing a stall door at the end of the aisle because someone had leaned against it so hard the hinge came loose. The horses who weren't sleeping, were searching their stalls for a piece of hay they had missed earlier and Keynote was busily churning fresh manure into his fresh bedding.

"Do you want to go to The Grill Girl for lunch and meet our new help? If you okay it, of course." Cap unclipped Spare from the cross ties.

"Sure."

I called Jules, told her we were going to town for lunch, and asked if she needed anything. She said no and Cap and I were off in the truck.

On the way she told me we were meeting Freddi Perino, who had graduated from Old Newbury High then spent a year at a hunter-jumper stable in Maryland and had come home looking for a similar situation. If she was pleasant and knew as much as Cap said she did, Freddi had a job.

The moment I met her, I knew she was a perfect fit for Tyr. As soon as we finished our hamburgers, the three of us returned to Bittersweet and Freddi got on Rosemary's gelding and rode him around the indoor.

It didn't take time or consideration. I gave her the job. Maybe now I would have fifteen minutes to myself each day and with that goal in mind, I tacked up CB, did the session Lockie had specified for us then took him out for a circuit around the pond.

The wind caused his mane to stand almost straight up and rattled the branches of the bare trees like skeletons dancing, but none of that made an impression on him. For all his training and all his breeding, CB was just a pet pony who could be ridden on the buckle.

When we reached the indoor, Poppy and Gincy were already mounted and warming up. I received a torrent of information on school gossip, books I had heard of and some I had never heard of and sounded too mature for them, and about the newest line of hoof print shirts available for spring shows. They careened from one topic to another without pausing to breathe. Poppy's mother, Aly, sat near the door laughing.

"Whoa," I said to them as I walked CB into the middle of the ring. "You have a show next month. Let's talk about that."

They cheered and immediately began deciding what classes they would enter even before looking at a prize list or hearing my plan for them.

I leaned over to CB's ears. "I have plans for us, too." I sat back up and said to the girls "Drop your stirrups and cross the leathers over your ponies' necks."

They groaned and I felt that I was doing my job.

***

It was frigid and tiny ice crystals were falling from the dark sky. Joly ran to me when I entered the kitchen and I picked him up for a snuggle and kiss.

"Where's Dad?"

Jules was sitting at the kitchen table, thumbing through a cookbook. "Wisconsin, where he is having a meeting with important people."

"We're not going to see very much of him this year," I replied.

"No, but your grandparents will be here."

Somehow that was not the comforting replacement it was intended to be. I loved them, but my feelings toward my father had changed so radically over the past months that when he wasn't at the farm, it felt like a loss.

"Do you like your father?" I sat down and put Joly in my lap.

"I both like him and love him."

"Always?"

Jules smiled. "He's a very strong personality so I didn't always agree with him but my family situation was much different than yours. Even though we were in Los Angeles, we lead a very normal life. You can work in the film industry without being a celebrity. As children, we had no fame, no notoriety and we had a very small allowance. Some of the girls at school had credit cards and went on shopping sprees. We didn't."

"What did you do for money? Don't take that the wrong way!"

Jules laughed. "No, I won't. As soon as possible, I got a job in a restaurant first as a waitress then as a hostess, then a prep chef."

"What does a prep chef do?"

"Cut vegetables for eight or ten hours."

"Awful."

"I loved it. I knew that if I could do that, working in a restaurant was in my future. After graduation, I went to Paris for two years. Then I went to Italy for two years. That was my college education. All I wanted was to be around food."

"You've never said why you didn't get a job in a restaurant."

"I discovered that cooking for strangers held no appeal for me. It's that simple."

"We..." I couldn't finish the sentence except in my mind. We would be lost without her.

Jules nodded. "Me, too. Go get ready for dinner. We'll make it a big deal for ourselves and I made a chicken thigh for Joly."

"Sounds good. I'll be back down in a few."

Joly and I went to my bedroom where I got out some clean clothes. Then my phone began ringing.

All afternoon I had been dreading this call. Any imaginary outcome would evaporate and what would be left would be real.

I clicked it on. "Hi."

"You're prepared for this?" Lockie asked.

"As much as I can be."

"I wish I was there with you but I'm here with you."

"I know."

"The horse was euthanized. There was internal bleeding and too much damage to repair."

I didn't say anything.

"These things happen. They can happen in the pasture."

"Should I point out they've never happened in my pasture."

"You haven't had a meteorite land in your pasture either, am I right?"

"Correct. How is Greer taking this?"

"I haven't seen Greer for hours."

This was not good.

As soon as I got off the phone with Lockie, I called Greer. It went to voice mail.

An hour later Lockie called to say he hadn't heard from her yet and had Tracy out trying to track her down.

I called Lockie at eight to say I hadn't heard from her.

At nine, we still hadn't heard anything.

By ten, I wanted to call the police and Jules talked me out of it.

Eleven came and went and I didn't even hear from Lockie.

"This is the last time she's allowed out of the house," I said to Jules, pacing back and forth in the den.

"Don't borrow trouble."

It was after midnight when the phone rang.

"Okay. I found her, she was with Cam," Lockie said.

By his tone of voice, I knew something was wrong beyond what we had already discussed.

"I'm sending her home tomorrow morning, so pick her up at Bradley. Teche doesn't have a shuttle going north."

"What do you mean she's coming home?"

There was a thunk, then Greer was on the phone crying. "He's just like everyone else..."

"Who?"

"Cam!"

I felt as though I had come into a theater in the middle of a play during the most dramatic scene with no idea what had happened during Act One. "What did he do?"

"He thinks I'm a saddle slut."

"What?"

I heard more noise on the phone, then Lockie got back on. "Apparently Cam suggested they sleep together. Sleep in the commonly understood usage of the word."

"Why?" I asked.

Had they been closer than I realized? Had they ever kissed? How did that happen between the serial arguments Cam and Greer had?

There was more struggling over the phone.

"Because he sleeps with everyone!" Greer shouted from a couple feet away.

I felt stupid. I didn't have enough pieces to put the puzzle together.

"She doesn't want to be here and I don't want her here like this. Overnight me my black boots, my show coat and my saddle."

"Why? Aren't you coming home with her?"

"I have a horse here. Counterpoint's supposed to show in jumpers, I'll show him. Your father has to get something out of this massive financial outlay."

"Lockie."

"It's all in my trunk. Call me after you've sent the box. Get it out before ten."

"Take your meds!" I shouted into the phone, and a moment later he had hung up.

9

EARLY THE NEXT MORNING, I opened his trunk in the tack room and found his show clothes stored in sealed plastic bags, his boot bag, and his good gloves. I put these in the truck along with his saddle in one of our Bittersweet Farm bags with CB nickering to me as I went past his stall. I assured him I would see him after lunch, but the kick at the stall door suggested he didn't believe me.

Greer's flight from Florida was arriving just before noon so I found an overnight shipper in Waterbury that I could get to easily before 10 a.m. as Lockie had instructed and make it to the airport in time. In a way, I didn't know what to expect. In a way, I did. Greer was capable of big emotions, anger for the most part, and tended to be at the top of the decibel level.

I didn't know why she was so angry with Cam and found what little I knew of the incident hard to believe. The show circuit was hardly comprised of celibates, but since he had been at Bittersweet Farm, I wasn't aware that Cam had dated anyone. The only person he had gone out with was Lockie. Maybe the winter show circuit was much different for Cam than living at his childhood home in Connecticut and it gave him permission to behave in a way I would find unrecognizable.

One thing I was sure of—I would hear about it all the way home from Bradley International Airport.

***

By the look of her, Greer had cried throughout the entire trip from Florida. Her eyes were red, her nose was red, and the only tissue she had left was a sodden mass. We picked up her luggage and saddle and went to my truck.

"It's freezing here," she said sitting in the passenger seat.

"It's winter." I started the engine.

We started for home and the only sound was that of the truck.

"Do you have any tissues?"

"Glove box," I replied.

Greer found the package and blew her nose.

"What happened?"

"Didn't Lockie tell you?"

"He told me to send his saddle and boots. I did. Why does he need them?" I replied.

"He's going to ride Counterpoint."

"I figured that much but why aren't you riding him?"

"Because Lockie sent me home."

I felt that we were going around in circles. "If you don't want to tell me, don't. I'm here to listen. I'll help you in any way I can. If you don't trust me or feel comfortable telling me, that's fine."

Greer started crying again. "He thought I would lay on my back for him."

"Cam?"

"Yes. And why not. That's what everyone thinks of me."

The only time I had heard anyone cry that hard was when I cried after my mother died.

"I'm only good for one thing," Greer managed to get out.

"That's not true—"

"—Don't tell anyone!"

"Even Jules?"

"NO ONE!"

"Whatever you want," I replied.

"What do you have to do to join the witness protection program?"

"I don't get it," I admitted.

"They give you a new life," Greer said simply.

***

Joly raced to Greer as we came in the door, she picked him up and was covered in puppy kisses.

"Did you eat on the way? Would you like something for lunch?" Jules asked as she turned a square of croissant dough and began rolling it out.

"No, thank you," Greer said as she headed for the stairs.

I sighed.

"Do you know what happened?"

"I was sworn to secrecy but what I've heard only makes tenuous sense."

"She was crying?"

"Oh yeah. Like a waterfall."

"I've never seen her cry."

"Nor have I. The pony riders have a lesson this afternoon so I need to get back to the barn."

"I'll go up and sit with her. Does Greer want to talk?"

"Nope. I think she just wants..."

"Tal, what?"

"A do-over for at least the last six years."

"We get a fresh start every morning."

I reached for the doorknob. "Can we convince her of that?"

Jules shrugged and I left the house.

It was better that Greer was home with us than in Florida. Lockie had made the right decision and obviously, she hadn't protested. Victoria hadn't made her life easy and never stopped trying to mold her daughter into Lady Greer Kensington-Rowe.

Greer was right. As far as I could tell, she was used by Victoria. It was something of a conversation piece to have a beautiful and accomplished daughter once the bloom was starting to go off the Victoria rose. Greer could help her mother navigate the society world more easily and make it understandable why Victoria appeared at functions perhaps not quite so age-appropriate.

It was all a muck-up and Greer didn't understand how much we cared about her. Maybe a visit from my grandmother would help. We could go to lunch in another town where there would be no chance we'd run into Victoria. The Garnet Inn. Greer could wear something pretty and I'd wear something that belonged to Jules as usual.

Entering the barn, I found Cap and Freddi, untacking Tyr and Spare.

"I know you have the pony riders in a while so we'll keep out of your way and hand-walk Whiskey and Call," Cap said. "I used the white board to improve the schedule Lockie sent. We'll be able to keep things straight that way."

"Thanks. I didn't think of that."

"You have other things on your mind." Cap was being far too generous.

Poppy and Gincy ran into the barn, braids bouncing as they came to me.

"Hi, Tal! I got an A on a paper I did about Lana duPont!" Gincy said. "I found her in a book after you told us about eventing."

"What about her," Freddi asked as she went to the tack room with a saddle.

"Lana duPont was the first woman to ride in the event competition at the Olympics," Gincy replied.

"And who did she ride," Cap asked.

"Mr. Wister!"

Freddi nodded. "That's right."

"Good for you, Gincy" I replied. "You're going to switch ponies today so go tack them up."

They were immobile. And plainly displeased.

"I don't want to ride Beau, no offense."

"I don't want to ride Tango, no offense, either," Gincy replied.

"Is this a mutiny?"

"Why can't I ride Tango?" Poppy asked.

"Because you both need experience riding other ponies and Call isn't available," I said. "You may find yourself in a show where you're asked to switch horses with another rider. You know that, right?"

The girls shrugged.

"It's true," Cap said.

"We all ride all the horses here at the farm," I added.

"Who else rides CB?"

"Lockie does. He showed him a couple months ago and took him to a dressage clinic. I ride Wingspread. That's part of what it means to be a good rider. You are able to ride any horse."

They both looked as though they didn't believe me.

"Okay. Think about it for as long as you need. Your lesson will be over at four no matter what happens. You've wasted about ten minutes so far, if you'd like to try to for fifteen, go ahead. I'll be cleaning tack until you decide." I turned and took a step away.

"All right, you win," Gincy said.

"Tack up the ponies and get on, I'll be right there," I replied.

They ran out of the barn.

"Nice," Freddi commented.

"You handled them really well," Cap remarked.

I nodded. If I could handle Greer so easily, I'd be set.

***

Chilled to the bone, I raced back to the house after the chores were done, and found Jules at the kitchen table surrounded by cookbooks.

"What are you doing?"

"I'm synthesizing a recipe for tomorrow's dinner. You father called and he'll be home with your grandparents, so I want to make it a special occasion."

"I thought you knew how to cook everything already."

"Not even close! See if you can send Greer down to set the table."

As I went to the stairs, that seemed like the least possible outcome. There wasn't a sound coming from her room and all the lights were off. I didn't want to wake her if she was asleep but if this was her way of limiting contact with the family, she could do that until my grandparents arrived. They had no conception of personal space or privacy. They were just what she needed.

As I was tying the laces on my formal paddock boots, my phone rang.

"Hi. I got your text messages. Thank you for letting me know Greer arrived in one wet piece."

"Yes, she's very upset."

"That's her choice."

"How...are you saying she should be happy right now?"

"Yes. She has nothing to be unhappy about."

"The horse died."

"It wasn't her horse. Tal, it's not an uncommon experience. I'm sorry, too, that the vets couldn't help him, but if it's any consolation, Nanci Huet is facing charges.

While her horse was being operated on, she was in the police station."

"Do expect me to feel sorry for her?"

"No, but that's hardly the issue facing us. I don't think we should get between Greer and Cam. He told me his version of what happened and I believe him."

"You disbelieve Greer," I asked in amazement.

"I didn't say that."

"Say something."

"Don't get mad at me. I had nothing to do with any of it," Lockie replied.

"If you're going to take sides against my sister—"

"That's not what I said. With everything going on, I think she did what she does best—overreact."

It was difficult if not impossible to come up with a logical argument against that statement.

"She belongs at home, where the world can be kept at arm's length."

"I don't know if that's fair," I said. Greer needed stability but not to be sequestered. That wouldn't last long even if it was attempted. She was the one who went to Florida, not me. It must have been an appealing opportunity to her, and the idea of showing every weekend for two months filled me with inertia.

"Okay. Will you come down to Napier next weekend? Watch me ride."

"Yes. I'll book the flight tomorrow."

If Greer had to take over for a few days, it would get her out of the bedroom and onto Citabria.

"I think Teche is coming in this direction. I'll let you know. Now I'm going to call it a day because this has been a long one."

"I know."

"And you don't have to shout at me to take my meds. My headache beat you to it."

***

We were doing a sitting trot around the indoor and while I should have been concentrating, I found my mind wandering. The volte at H was missed and I didn't even realize it until I got to K.

"He really is perfect for you."

Shifting my weight, CB walked and I turned to Greer. "It's like I'm in kindergarten and he's a PhD."

"What's wrong with that? He'll teach you, or drag you, whatever is necessary."

"Are you going back to Florida?" I asked going to her.

"No."

"Are you going to continue showing?"

"I just had a really bad week, Tal, do I need to know my lifeplan today?"

"I'm asking for a selfish reason. I need your help on a little project."

Greer looked at me without enthusiasm.

"Don't go back to your bedroom. I need help. There's a show at Swingletree Farm at the end of the month."

"I don't have anyone to ride."

"I want to ride."

"What?"

"I don't necessarily want to, but going in the baby dressage class is what I was thinking of."

"You could probably be sound asleep and he could get you through the test," Greer remarked.

"I have never gone to a show where there was no pressure on me and if this is a more casual sort of attempt that doesn't require hanging around all day—"

"–Watching me win–"

"Exactly. Maybe I'll feel differently."

"Why don't you go with Cap?"

"I want it to be a stealth show. I don't want anyone to know so when I make an idiot of myself I'm not embarrassed."

"You want me to be your groom?"

"No. I want you to be my sister."

Greer thought for a moment. "Are we taking the van?"

"Let's take Lockie's trailer."

113

10

WHEN WE GOT BACK to the house, my father and grandparents had arrived from the city. I was silently praying "Make a fuss over Greer but not too much."

They were smarter than I gave them credit for, making a fuss over both of us, but didn't mention Florida once. My grandmother wanted to know all about the Ambassador of Good Cheer, and what the next step would be on that project.

Surprising me, Greer had answers. Not only had she kept current while away, she made plans. With Valentine's Day coming up next month, several appearances had been arranged for Trish and Oliver. The Christmas season had been so successful that there were inquiries from other organizations and groups wanting Trish and Oliver to visit them.

My grandparents couldn't have been more proud of Greer and there was so much excitement over her that Joly started dashing around the room, barking and jumping. Grabbing him before he made too much of a pest of himself, I took him outside for a whizz.

Standing outside to give Greer a chance to be the center of attention, I could see Butch and the ponies in their field. For those few minutes, it was so peaceful.

Then my phone rang.

"Hi."

"Hi. I got the box. Thank you."

"You're welcome."

"There will be living streaming vid of the class I'm riding in tomorrow," Lockie said. "So don't miss it."

"Okay."

"I managed to get the secretary to change Counterpoint from ami-owner. It didn't make them very happy since the programs are printed already and list has gone out to the broadcast company—"

"But you were very convincing."

"I must have been," Lockie replied. "How is Greer?"

"My grandparents came up for a visit so she's telling them all about Oliver and Trish. I'm out here in the cold with Joly."

"Do you think she'll be upset to see me ride Counterpoint?"

"I think that's the least of her concerns at the moment."

"Will you be upset?" He asked.

"What do you think?"

"That's too long to hold your breath. I'll be fine. Counterpoint is a terrific horse. The fences aren't anything that tests his abilities. He's very careful and wants to go clean. I'll just be a passenger."

Who would believe that about Lockie?

***

I was in bed reading when Greer tapped on the door and came in with Joly.

"What's going on?" I asked when she didn't say anything.

"Would you scrunch over?"

I moved and she got in beside me putting Joly between us.

"I hate it that the Huet horse died."

"It upset me, too."

Greer didn't say anything for a long moment. "I don't know what to do."

"About what?"

"Anything. Everything."

"All that won't fit on your plate. Just take it in small increments. The rest of today, then tomorrow morning,

116

then lunch, then the afternoon. You can help me with the Zuckerlumpens or whatever Lockie called them."

"What?"

"Sugar Lumps. The pony riders. I nearly had a revolt before the last lesson. I asked them to switch ponies. You would have thought it would result in the earth cracking apart into large chunks, and casting us helplessly adrift in the dark void of space."

"Would you let me ride CB?"

"Of course. Ride him tomorrow."

"You treat me better than I treated you."

"That's in the past."

Greer didn't say anything for a couple minutes. "I came around the corner of the barn, walking Counterpoint to cool him out and saw her beating her horse. I saw blood on the crop. I told her to stop, that I could see blood. And she smiled at me and said 'That's tomato soup.' I wanted to tear Nanci 'I'm a Monster and Proud of It' Huet's head off."

I squeezed her hand as the tears fell.

***

"I can't ride this horse," Greer said as she turned CB to the center of the ring.

"What do you mean?"

117

"He's like a bumper car!"

I shook my head.

"He's all over the place. How do you ride him?"

I had to try to translate what she was saying before replying. "Lockie has trouble with him too."

"That can't be possible."

I pulled a piece of carrot from my jacket pocket and offered it to him.

Greer slid off. "Ride him around and let me see what he does with you."

She handed me her helmet and gave me a leg up.

I headed toward the track at a trot. We went around once then switched directions, then cantered in the opposite direction on a loose rein. We transitioned into a trot as I picked up contact with his mouth then we performed a shoulder-in then a half-pass at the opposite side of the indoor. I dropped the reins and patted his neck with both hands.

"It's me," Greer said.

"He's a little eccentric," I admitted.

"Why doesn't he like me?"

"He doesn't know you. You have to let us know you, Greer." I slid off to the ground and began running up my irons.

"What if you don't like me?"

"Because we liked the other Greer so much more?"

We walked out of the indoor together.

118

"People aren't like horses."

"That's true," I replied.

"Horses are honest. They don't hide their feelings. If they want to kick you, they kick you. People will wait for the most opportune moment, and then they kick you."

I put my hand on CB's neck. "Not all people. Give us a chance."

Greer didn't reply.

***

When we entered the kitchen, my grandmother turned away from lunch preparations to hug us.

"Your face is so cold," she told Greer. "Take a hot shower."

"I'll be fine," Greer said. "Where's Joly?"

"On my lap," my grandfather said with a smile. "He's very personable."

"Maybe we'll get a dog," my grandmother said.

"Not with all the traveling you do," my father replied from his seat at the kitchen table. "You'll just leave it here for us to take care of."

"We'll borrow Mr. Joly then, when we visit," my grandfather said as he handed the puppy to Greer. "If that's okay with you."

"Sure." Greer put Joly on the floor and went to get his lunch.

I washed up at the sink. "In about an hour, Lockie's going to be not exactly on television but close."

"Really? How?"

"It will be live streaming video on the Internet starting after the lunch break."

"I'm confused." My grandmother sat down next to Greer. "Will we be able to watch it on the television or must we hunch over the computer?"

"The class can be viewed on the television but it will be unbelievably boring for you," I replied.

Greer nodded. "We'll call you when there are a few horses ahead of him instead of fifty, then it won't be so bad."

"We'll all watch," my father said and began to eat lunch.

***

An hour later, Greer and I were in the den watching horse after horse jump the course and Lockie hadn't even made it to the list yet. She explained how she wanted a group of four Ambassador of Cheer teams by the summer so they could appear at town fairs on a rotating basis. That way, the responsibility wouldn't only be on Trish and Oliver.

"I don't know how you're going to duplicate Oliver. He's such a performer," I replied.

"Trish can share her knowledge with the other participants. I'm sure each dog will have a talent that can be featured."

"Even to run through a companion dog test where they sit and stay or retrieve is quite entertaining since most dogs can't do anything but stare at you hopefully while you eat."

"Exactly. These are 4-H members. Their dogs are trained." Greer looked down at Joly. "Unlike you."

He wagged his tail.

On the broadcast, the commentator gave his analysis of the last round, and said there were eleven riders left.

I looked up at the screen and Lockie was the sixth from the last. Jennifer Nicholson was after him riding one of Teche's horses, Roux.

"She's really a piece of work," Greer said glancing up at the list. "I guess she's a good enough, but she's getting by on a small talent."

"How so?"

"If you see her ride at the same time as Lockie, the difference is obvious. Jennifer is not a smart girl." Greer left the room to get the others.

The less I thought about Jennifer, the better it was for me. The less Jennifer thought about Lockie, the better it was for him. She seemed to think that because they had dated once upon a time, that history meant something.

Maybe she flirted with every male, and that was just her personality and she couldn't turn it off. If so, it was a shame that Jennifer didn't know what a caricature she had become. It was like watching a bad situation comedy to see her in action.

I wondered how Jennifer would do in this class. A tight three-element combination had left a number of the horses with rails down. For those who went clean and fast, there was a good chance at placing, even winning the class. That was Jennifer's style according to Lockie. Anyone who rode a conservative round was out of the ribbons.

I didn't know what Lockie's choice would be. Besides the dressage class on CB, I had never seen him show. Since this was his first time out with Counterpoint, would he want to put in a clean round and be satisfied? Or the other option was to do what he had done before switching to eventing. Lockie had been a catch rider. He went to shows and people would have him ride horses he hadn't be on before. The point was to win or at the very least, do as best as the horse could do. That meant pushing.

People took showing very seriously, either as a matter of pride or money. A horse who won was more valuable to an owner than one who didn't place.

It required a certain mindset, one that I didn't have, to see horses or people as valuable based on their performance. All I wanted was for Lockie and Counterpoint to make it around without hurting themselves and didn't care how slow they went in order to achieve that. Unfortunately, that was not the point of this sport.

Greer returned with everyone else and we all waited impatiently for Lockie to go.

The gate opened and he and Counterpoint entered the ring. The camera didn't go in for a close-up but Lockie still looked more elegant than anyone else.

Trotting, he made a large circle between jumps to show Counterpoint the course, then began to canter and headed for the first fence. They were all verticals. What wasn't a vertical was an oxer. All of them looked like something horses were supposed to stay on the other side of, not go over.

I remembered Lockie told me to breathe, but I couldn't. It didn't help that my grandparents were gasping and exclaiming with each fence.

Standing to my side, Greer put her hand on my shoulder. "He's fine," she whispered.

Lockie and Counterpoint took the combination, made a tight turn for the last line and then their round was over.

"Breathe," Greer told me.

"Wasn't that something," my grandfather said. "I've never seen anything like it."

"He's a fine rider," my father replied.

Ever ready with the business advice, my grandfather looked at him. "Don't let him get away."

"I think there's very little chance of that, Dad."

"Are they done?" My grandmother asked.

"I hope so," I said.

Jules stood. "Would anyone like a little nosh?"

"There's always room for a little something." My grandmother followed Jules to the kitchen.

Greer sat next to me. "Now for Jennifer."

The gate opened and Jennifer rode in on Teche's big chestnut with a lot of chrome. She trotted around the way everyone else had, then steered for the first fence.

"This is what's wrong with her," Greer commented. "She's loose."

"Hmmm," I replied.

Roux landed and Jennifer was pitched forward as they galloped toward the second fence.

"Choose if you're going to sit in the saddle or not, sweetie," Greer said to the television.

They cleared the second fence with Jennifer hanging onto the horse's mouth and he threw his head in the air to get away from her. I didn't blame him.

They cleared the next three fences and were confronted with what was already a sharp turn. Jennifer spurred him on and pulled him tighter. Roux's hind legs went out from under him and he fell on his flank. Jennifer was left in the dirt as the horse ran off.

A moment later, Lockie and Counterpoint galloped across the ring, followed by Cam on foot.

Jennifer wasn't getting up and now the ground crew was running toward her.

"Would everyone clear the ring." The show announcer called over the public address system.

Lockie reached her first and leaped off Counterpoint to crouch next to her.

"Oh my god," Greer groaned.

Cam arrived at the scene as Jennifer was attempting to stand.

That the announcer was begging for people to move back and give her room didn't make the least impression on Cam and Lockie. Counterpoint had no choice but to stand there, completely in the way.

The paramedics arrived and the video of Jennifer was replaced by a panoramic view of the show grounds.

"Who says chivalry isn't dead?" Greer stood. "How many more of her former or current dates, and I use that term loosely, but not as loose as she is, are going to come running out of the stable area to her side? What a saddle slut!" She slapped her hand on her thigh and Joly followed Greer out of the den.

My father looked at me.

"His ex," I said.

"Believe him," he replied.

I nodded and left the room.

***

My grandmother and grandfather dragged Greer into a round of their favorite game of dice after dinner. It was not that I didn't want to play or be part of the excitement of rolling five 6's, it was that I wanted Greer to be with them. While it wasn't nearly as stimulating as going to Sabine's house, and doing whatever she used to do there, her former friend was long off the radar. This kind of activity was better for her and probably nothing she had ever done with the Kensington-Rowe side of the family tree.

The best thing that Greer could do was disinherit those people. They had never been a stabilizing influence and obviously had raised Greer's mother in the exact same manner, which accounted for why Victoria was so unconcerned with her daughter unless it benefitted her in some way.

After taking a shower, I got in bed early, fully determined to catch up on my reading but found myself replaying Jennifer's accident. When is an accident not an accident, I wondered. Her fearless attitude and her lack of stickability to the saddle bothered me at the approach to the first fence. Instead of helping the horse, I felt as though she was making it harder for him by not being able to keep her balance.

I knew Jennifer had won many classes at some of the largest competitions in the country and was considered one of the top show jumpers on the circuit. With no background in that division, it was unfair of me to judge her. Perhaps it was just an accident. The horse might have stepped wrong and went down. Horses fall often enough, with nothing more than a bruise or a sprain as a result. The rider usually spits out dirt for the rest of the day.

Or, in the case of Lockie's accident, broken bones, a bruised brain, light and sound sensitivity and memory loss. He had been so lucky that was all that happened to him.

My phone rang and I clicked it on.

"Hi."

"Can you come down before the weekend? Thursday."

"Of course."

"It won't be with Teche. I found someone else who will give you a ride. You have to go to Dutchess County Airport, is that okay?"

I had no idea where that airport was, but it had to be on a map. "Just tell me when and Greer or Cap will drive me over."

There was silence.

"Lockie?"

"Counterpoint came in fourth. Did you know that?"

"Good for you! Yes, I'm sorry I didn't congratulate you. We all quit watching after Jennifer's accident but I found the results on the Internet. Is she all right?"

"I just got back from the hospital. When she started to fall, I could see her arm was out. You have to let yourself fall and roll."

"If you have the presence of mind." Usually I went splat on the ground and lay there until my lungs began working again.

"The orthopedic surgeons had to rebuild her elbow. All the bones in her arm were broken."

"Jennifer really hit the ground wrong," I said.

"I know you probably saw it on the live stream."

"Greer, Jules, my father, and my grandparents watched it on the television."

"It would have been better if you didn't see it."

"Yes. Greer reacted as you might expect."

"How did you react?"

"As you might expect."

"Silly."

"I never saw anyone ride more beautifully than you did."

"Thursday can't come fast enough," he said.

He was right.

11

ON THURSDAY MORNING, I waved goodbye to Greer and went up the steps of the Gulfstream III parked on the ramp at Dutchess County Airport. I didn't know what to expect and only knew the family's name was Saunders.

"Hi! I'm glad I don't have to make the trip alone. It's always better to have someone to talk to, don't you think?"

So small in the large seat, the girl couldn't have been more than eleven.

"I do. I'm Talia Margolin. Thank you for the ride."

"I'm Ryan Saunders. I just got out of school for the week and now I can go down to ride my pony, Sideshow Ding."

"Cute name. Are you meeting your parents in Florida?"

She shook her head. "No. My mother is based in Paris and my father is working on a movie. They're divorced."

"I'm sorry."

"I'm not. They started to hate each other."

No child should have that burden and Greer was testament to that, having barely survived her parents' relationship.

"Who are you staying with in Florida?" I asked as the flight attendant closed the door and the jet began to roll toward the taxiway.

"My trainer found me a room."

Don't anyone go out of their way to make it nice for this kid. Leave her in Florida on her own, in a room at a motel or something. What kind of madness was this?

Taking out a piece of paper from my bag, I wrote down my cell phone number and Teche's stable name. "If you need some help or company over the weekend, call me or you can call the barn. They'll be able to find me."

"Thank you, Talia. I'm very self-sufficient," Ryan replied.

That didn't surprise me in the least.

About three hours later, we landed in Florida. A town car was there to take Ryan to her trainer, and Lockie, tan and leaner than usual, was standing in the terminal waiting for me.

I wanted to hold him close but we had a prohibition about touching each other in public. The appearance must be of a completely professional relationship. Lockie was the trainer at Bittersweet Farm, and there must not be the slightest hint of anything else even a friendship.

As much as I regretted that, at least we were in the same state.

Lockie helped me with the bags, and we got in the car to drive to Acadiana South. Florida was as flat as I remembered it. It was also warm and lush with green grass, palm trees, and colorful flowers in profusion. When he turned into the driveway and the automatic gate opened, I was sure we were at a country club or exclusive hotel. The house was huge and so were the paddocks. Then to one side there was an enormous outside course on grass, after that was a ring with footing that had recently been dragged.

"Do you want to go to your room first or the barn?"

"The barn. Is it going to be a shock?"

Lockie nodded. "Probably, if you haven't been to a comparable stable."

"There are more farms like this?" I asked.

"Many and within walking distance." He stopped the car in front of the stable and we got out.

I had not taken two strides inside the building when I came to a complete halt.

"There are chandeliers in the barn."

"Not crystal ones," Lockie replied.

It was magnificent. Every surface was polished and shining. There wasn't a speck of hay or bedding on the aisle and the temperature was perfect. The coats of the horses glistened to a high sheen.

"This makes Bittersweet Farm look like a dairy barn," I commented as we went down the aisle.

"That's not true. Bittersweet is a home. This is a ridiculous display that adds nothing of substance."

I turned to him. "Do you really think so?"

"Yes. This is a rental. Does Acadiana Farm in Connecticut look anything like this?"

"No."

"Teche has a good time with this over-the-top grandeur. It's fun for him to invite guests, throw parties, and use his spice mixes on the food while he's here. Don't forget his roots in the swamp. This isn't more real for him than it is for us. People talk, he gets his name around, gets his picture in the local paper. It's publicity. Who would gossip if you came here with a dollar horse and a homebuilt trailer?" Lockie asked.

"No one, I suppose."

"No one."

We stopped at Counterpoint's stall and he came over to us. I had a small bag of horse cookies in my bag and opened it to give him one. The crunching alerted the horses around him to the fact that someone was eating between meals and one began nudging the wall with his front hoof.

"Are you ready for this show?"

"Sure. Are you worried?"

"No."

"Tell the truth," Lockie said.

"I'm not having nightmares about it like I would if you were going cross country."

"We'll be fine. He's a very good horse."

I gave Counterpoint another cookie.

"Is Greer upset that I placed on him and she didn't?"

"I don't think it really occurred to her. She knows you're a better rider than she is."

"Now."

I kissed Counterpoint's nose.

"Greer doesn't ride up to her skill level. Someday she will."

We began walking out of the barn through the rear exit.

"It was quite a situation you found yourself in. One sister who is like a stick of dynamite with the fuse lit and the other like a stick of dynamite that's been soaking in a water bucket. There must have been evenings when you sat on the ugliest couch in the world wondering how you got to Bittersweet Farm."

"I sure did."

We stepped into what was left of the daylight.

"I thought how did I get so lucky," Lockie continued.

"You don't have to be polite. We're past that by now."

"Point number one, we're not past that and will never be. Point number two, I was always very grateful."

"But you belong here."

"I belong at home, but I have business to do for the farm here. Just like your father travels for Swope."

"Besides the two grooms from Teche, and Cap, I had to hire someone part-time because there wasn't enough help once Zuckerlumpens moved in."

Lockie laughed. "*Zuckerwuerfel.*"

"Right. Them, too. You can't imagine the vacuum you create when you go."

"But you feel that way about your father now, too, don't you?"

I thought for a moment. "Yes."

"I'm glad."

We went up the walkway to the house and I was bracing myself for more over-the-top ostentatious interior design. Lockie opened the door and I was not unprepared, but still shocked. How could anyone call this home? But I imagined that if that's what you knew, it might be. Or if someone had grown up with bayou alligators strolling in through the backdoor, this would be palatial. The foyer was polished marble and the color scheme reflected the natural colors of Florida--sunbleached everything.

"You're staying in the house, and Cam and I are in one of the guest houses."

Nodding, I tried to take all this splendor of new wealth in.

"We'll go out to dinner tonight, the three of us."

"Lockie—"

He shrugged.

***

Before going out to dinner, I called Greer from her old/exceedingly new room.

"It's depressing," I said.

"The Teche Homestead? It's nothing like the Kensington-Rowe country house, I can assure you of that," Greer replied. "After being lived in for five hundred years, everything in that house is frayed, stained, or rubbed raw. And now, there's the great pleasure of tourists traipsing through instead of the Roundheads. 'Oh look, Petunia! This is just like the house in *Mansfield Park*. The wall is cracking in the corner of the bedroom, too.'"

"Is it just like the house in the movie?"

"It is the house they used in the movie. Do you think my grandparents would turn money down?"

"If I say no, will it hurt your feelings?"

Greer almost laughed. "They used the money to stay in Saint-Paul-de-Vence for the duration instead of fixing the cracked wall. Hurt my feelings? No. I know them. There is nothing you can say about that side of the family that I haven't said already."

"That's okay. You're a Swope."

"You're not," Greer replied.

That was true since I kept my mother's name after the marriage. "Genetically, I'm a Swope as much as you are."

"I've got the name to prove it," Greer said.

By now, I knew her well enough to believe she was teasing me. "Only when you don't need to be minor royalty. Then suddenly you become Mistress Kensington-Rowe and cut to the front of the line."

"I learned from the masters. How's my horse?"

"I saw Counterpoint about an hour ago and gave him the cookies you sent with me. He's fine, living like a princeling in a castle with chandeliers."

"We might as well leave him there. He'll be embarrassed to live in a normal barn after this."

"I think he'd prefer to be with you," I said truthfully.

"He'd prefer being with Lockie."

"Don't we all?"

"I had an idea for another video."

"No more videos."

"This is good," Greer said. "How not to let your pony stand on your foot."

I groaned, imagining what happened to put that idea in her head.

***

Cam and Lockie were waiting for me by the car.

"I'm driving," Cam said.

Of course he was. Lockie didn't drive at night and I didn't know where the restaurant was.

"You get in the front and I'll sit in the back," Lockie said.

I opened the door. "I flew fifteen hundred miles for this? I can't even sit with you in the backseat?"

"No."

I pulled the door shut, hard, and Lockie got in the back.

"Hi, Tal," Cam said as he slid behind the steering wheel.

"You're not my choice of the optimal dinner companion," I replied.

"Ouch," Cam said as we drove through the automatic gate and it closed behind us.

After driving into the center of Napier, Cam parked at a bistro, we got out and walked to the front door overhung by a striped awning and bracketed by two boxwood topiaries.

This was not how I imagined my first night in Florida would be. Even if we ate at a hamburger stand, I thought we would find a way to be a twosome. I certainly didn't want to be a threesome with Cam. My interest in dinner had dissipated entirely.

We were greeted by a hostess, and since Lockie had made a reservation, were brought to a table on the terrace lit by fairy lights and lanterns to heighten the sense of exclusivity. It might have been dark, but every table had customers so we were hardly alone. Lockie pulled out the chair for me, I sat down, and he pushed me assertively toward the table, which I took as a hint to behave.

"So." The menu was handed to me by a waiter. "Florida."

"Yes."

"Are there any alligators in the bushes?"

Cam smiled. "If there were, Teche would have barbecued them already."

I didn't want to be polite to him. He had hurt Greer's feeling to such a degree that she had come home. Greer didn't leave shows. She liked the atmosphere, the horses, riders and action. To have Cam touch a nerve with her, however it happened, was unprecedented.

Ordering the least amount possible, I handed the menu back to the waiter and felt Lockie's foot nudge mine under the table.

"What will it take to get over this scratchy feeling between some of us?" Lockie asked.

"I don't want to get past it," I replied.

"I do," Cam said.

"Of course you do. You don't think you did anything wrong."

"I didn't do anything wrong."

"There ya go. Avoid taking responsibility at all cost," I replied.

"I'm not avoiding it," Cam said.

Lockie put his hand down on the table. "We're not going to argue over dinner."

"Later then," I said.

There was a moment of silence, then a man came up between us. "Excuse me. I'm sorry to interrupt your meal but I didn't want the opportunity to get away. I'm Ed D'Angelis, and I saw you ride in the jumper class, Lockie. I asked around, and it's said you will ride for people. There's a horse in my barn I would like you to ride."

Lockie pushed back his chair and stood. "Excuse me while I go talk to Mr. D'Angelis. Please play nice while I'm gone."

I waited until Lockie couldn't hear me and leaned over to Cam. "What you did to Greer was unforgiveable!"

"What did I do?"

"You think she's..."

"What?" Cam asked. "What do I think she is?"

"You heard about Rui."

"Everyone on the circuit has heard about Rui because he can't keep quiet about any of his conquests."

"See. Conquest! You thought you could do the same."

Cam said nothing.

"I can't tell you how deeply you hurt her feelings. I picked her up at Bradley and she cried all the way home."

"Maybe I was inelegant but Greer was so upset, I just wanted to comfort her."

Did I hear him correctly? "You proposition her as a comfort gesture?"

"That's what men do. We're not girls. Giving a stuffed animal and a cute greeting card is not the go-to solution."

"So sex is?"

"It's very life-affirming."

"You know the first rule of holes? Step away from the shovel and stop digging."

"I thought she needed someone to be close to."

"So give her a hug!"

"I've been watching her for weeks. Greer acts like an abused horse. I don't know what happened to her, but she's not getting past it. No matter what your opinion is about me, I care about her."

I stopped. "What do you mean abused?"

"What's the word mean to you? Haven't you ever wondered why Greer is the way she is? Did you just think she was in a bad mood?"

I couldn't speak as our lives fast forwarded through my mind.

"You did," Cam said. "There's more to it than being a bitch. Some incident or incidents are the cause. And seeing that horse beaten must have brought it back to her. She couldn't maintain the façade anymore. I bet she still hasn't told you."

I shook my head.

"Let her do it in her own time but now you know. I'm sorry I hurt her feelings. That wasn't my intention."

The waiter put my dinner in front of me, then Cam's. "Should I take the other entrée back to the kitchen?"

Dinner had gone to hell.

***

After the meal, Cam left us off at the main house and went to the cottage he shared with Lockie. We walked to the barn to check Counterpoint for the night. I was still reeling from what had transpired over dinner.

"Cam told you."

"Yes."

"He said he would."

We stopped at Counterpoint's door and I turned to Lockie. "You believe him?"

"Yes. I'm sorry I never put all the pieces together."

"You have nothing to regret. You are always kind to her. I fought with her for years."

"Greer can be a tough cookie," Lockie replied.

"What do I do now?" I opened the stall door, put my arms around Counterpoint's neck and breathed in his scent. "I should tell my father."

"I won't tell you what you should or should not do."

"What do you think we should do?"

"It's Greer's life to live and her secrets to keep or reveal."

"You think that's the best?"

"Yes. If she's not ready for people to know, it's not our decision to make. Cam knew. He could have chosen that moment to confront her but he—"

"If Cam knows so much about her, didn't it cross his mind that she might take the proposition the wrong way?"

Lockie shrugged. "So we're a little bit clumsy at the wrong times. This isn't a chick flick where the guy knows just the right thing to say."

"But sex? At a time like that?"

"Made sense to me," Lockie replied. "He was there for her and still is. That must count for something."

I kissed Counterpoint instead of Lockie.

12

BREAKFAST WAS SERVED buffet style at Acadiana, with a wide choice of Cajun, Southern and predictable offerings. Teche was in Louisiana on business as was standard during the week and he returned to Florida if his horses were competing.

Since Jennifer's accident made it impossible for her to ride for the foreseeable future, she had gone to her parents' home in Arizona to recuperate. I was not happy she had been hurt, but pleased my visit didn't mean I'd see her again.

Someone had to ride the horses she was scheduled to show and given that he was already on the property, Teche had asked Lockie to take over. I was both pleased and concerned. He wanted to get back on the circuit, of course, but I didn't want him to overdo the amount of riding

143

required. Plus, now he had agreed to help Ed D'Angelis out this weekend.

Which was why by mid-morning, I found myself on Counterpoint while Lockie rode Roux and Cam spotted for us on the ground. After warming up, we did some work on the flat, flexibility exercises, yielding for Roux more than Counterpoint who had already been through Lockie's program. Roux was accustomed to Jennifer's normal style of galloping to every fence and throwing herself on his neck while hoping for the best. Cam set up a serpentine of rails on the ground interspersed with a couple low, plain rail fences much like we had trained over at home. It was no problem for Counterpoint but Roux had difficulty bending and didn't understand he wasn't supposed to rush.

The moment we dismounted, grooms were there to take care of the horses and handed Lockie the reins of Tabiche, another of Jennifer's former rides. There was nothing for me to do but stand at the rail and watch two professionals fine tune for the upcoming classes.

With Cam's focus on show jumping, he had a depth of experience and knowledge that surprised me. In the most efficient manner, he was able to communicate what needed to be done and was his usual sunny self. Both he and Lockie enjoyed what they were doing and loved horses.

My phone rang and I hoped it wasn't Greer. If it was, I would let it go to voicemail and call her later. By caller ID, I could see it was the house phone and for a moment I didn't know what to do. I decided if it was Greer, tell her the truth almost entirely and say we were exercising horses and I'd call her in the afternoon.

"Hi."

"Dolcezza," Jules said to me.

"Good."

"Excuse me?"

"I'm glad to hear from you."

"What's wrong," she asked.

"Everything is complicated here. Maybe I should have stayed home." I replied, then watched as Lockie cantered the dark red horse easily around the ring. "No, but it would have been easier."

"Are you all right? Is Lockie all right?"

"Lockie is doing exactly what he should be. He's riding for Teche now because Jennifer went home. Someone came up to us at dinner last night and practically begged him to ride his horse. We're going to that stable in a while."

"How do you feel about that?"

I stepped away from the ring so the conversation wouldn't distract Lockie or Tabiche. "I don't want him to overdo it and I'm not sure he's taking care of himself. This is quite a bit of exertion."

"That's very sweet of you but I think Lockie can decide when he's tired."

In the ring, Cam was raising a couple of the fences as Lockie trotted Tabiche, who was sharp and full of himself, on the track, getting deep into the corners.

"He decides too late. His gauge needs to be recalibrated," I told her. "How are things there?"

"If you mean Greer, she has been huddled with Amanda over the Ambassador of Cheer project. The question du jour was how to go about increasing production of Oliver popcorn balls."

I had to try to shift gears. "Is Oliver our logo?"

"I don't know if it's specifically Oliver. How close a representation of any dog can a popcorn ball be?"

"What if Trish quits?" I wanted to avoid saying what if Oliver is no longer available. "Then do you need to model a different dog?"

"No," Jules replied.

"Aren't the church ladies sufficient?"

"According to Greer, no, because she was informed they are planning the Newbury beautification campaign and can't devote their time to our cheer. Their cheer will be taking up their time."

"Let's find some other church ladies or their equivalent. It's a charitable project. Someone should be available to help. The Girl Scouts?"

"I think Greer wants to put the popcorn balls into grocery stores," Jules said.

"For sale?" This idea blindsided me. I wasn't aware there was an unfilled niche for popcorn balls in the food world.

"Yes, with the proceeds going to the charity which in turn will train more Oliver clones."

"No, I don't want to do this."

"Take it up with your sister. She's going full steam ahead."

Then I was happy for her.

A shadow fell across my face and I looked up to see Lockie on Tabiche standing next to me.

"We have to go to see Ed D'Angelis," Lockie reminded me.

"Right. Bye, Jules, I'll call you later."

"Bye, sweetie."

I clicked off the phone. "Ready to go when you are."

The groom was holding Tropizienne for Cam and took Tabiche's reins the moment Lockie dismounted.

"See you later," Cam said as he turned the horse for the ring.

"Dinner?" I asked as we headed to the car.

"If you'd like."

I nodded.

We didn't have a chaperone on the trip to the D'Angelis stable.

Lockie would have one opportunity to ride the horse before getting to the show grounds in Napier tomorrow morning. It was not something I would be comfortable doing but it was normal for him. To be fair to myself, I had ridden very few horses compared to Lockie. Most of my experience had been on Butch. I had never ridden Greer's equitation horse, Sans Egal, while she was still showing him. Then I got CB who treated me very well. All the horses at Bittersweet were quiet and uncomplicated, even Lockie's horse, Wingspread, was capable of trotting me around in a most relaxed way.

The world was not full of horses like that. Before Lockie arrived, the last horse I had ridden off the farm had stood up with me. I did not enjoy the sense I was a Wild West cowgirl on a bronco, rearing and plunging around the yard. It was no small wonder why I didn't want to ride any horse but Butch for years.

"Tal? Why are you so quiet? Are you still upset over Greer?"

"No, you were right. Pretty much. Cam had the right instinct but the wrong choice of how to reach Greer."

"As is so common with her."

"She can be a handful," I admitted.

"You had the wind under your tail last night at dinner, too."

"Sorry. I should have given Cam a chance to explain and then bit his head off."

Lockie smiled.

"How many people have asked you to ride horses for them?" I asked.

"The only one I said yes to was Ed D'Angelis."

"Why him and not the others?"

"The horse sounded interesting. It's a coming six German gelding who is quiet until he throws in a buck between fences."

"Jumper?"

"Hunter."

"That's not good. Why would a horse do that?"

Judges didn't want to see fireworks from a hunter. They were supposed to be well-mannered, quiet, able to go on a looser rein and definitely not act like they would kick a hound that got behind them on the hunt field.

"There are a lot of reasons horses don't do what we'd like them to do. They have their own opinions and agenda. Like CB with his swish. They're our partners not our subjects."

"I don't want to see a horse so well-behaved, whatever that means, that he has no personality," I said.

Lockie turned the car into the driveway. "You're cute, Silly."

The barn was off to the left side of the property and the house was directly at the end of the driveway. It was a smaller house, by far, than Teche's rented estate but impressive with the appearance of a Spanish hacienda surrounded by tall palm trees. It was lovely and probably quite expensive given the desirability of land at the center of the Florida show horse world.

As we drove up, the front door opened, and Mr. D'Angelis came out to greet us. "We can drive up to the barn," he said and got in the back seat.

Lockie continued down the gravel way. "Ed, this is Talia Margolin from Bittersweet Farm. My boss, one might say."

I was not one who would say that. My father was the boss of everyone and we all knew it.

"I'm very pleased to meet you," Ed said. "Thank you for loaning Lockie to me for the weekend."

"He does make his own decisions and if he wants to wear the seat of his breeches threadbare while he's in Florida, that's his choice."

Ed laughed as we pulled up to the barn and got out.

It was a barn not much larger than the one at home, but newer, shinier and the aisle was easily wide enough to accept a pickup truck. We could fit the farm tractor in our barn and normally just parked it in the doorway where we loaded the bucket with soiled bedding twice a day.

A large black horse with a white snip on his nose, was cross tied and being tacked by a groom.

"I had an agent buy Kyffhäuser in Germany for me last summer as a prospect and sent him to a trainer in New Jersey. It didn't work out as I hoped. He seems like a nice horse but then he has his moments. Usually at the worst time," Ed told us.

Lockie put his own saddle on the horse and went to rub his forehead.

I knew what Lockie was silently saying to the horse. "What's your story?"

We went out the back exit to the large paddocks off to one side and a ring to the other, while Ed listed Kyffhäuser's indiscretions. I started to feel sorry for the horse who seemed to have a dunce cap permanently attached to his crownpiece.

I held the off side stirrup while Lockie got on from the mounting block and went into the ring.

Although he was a beautiful horse, Kyffhäuser seemed unhappy to me. His resistance came in small, but definitive ways from the moment he was asked to trot. His ears weren't pricked forward, his tail swished back and forth, he was stiff, unyielding and after a low three fence combination, threw in a buck.

Lockie let the reins go slack, gave him a couple pats on the neck, and brought the gelding over to us.

"You have other horses in the barn. I know you've invested time and money to bring them here, but showing Kyffhäuser this weekend will be counterproductive." Lockie dismounted and ran up his irons.

"This is supposed to be a well-trained horse. I paid top dollar for him."

I didn't know how well-trained a German horse would be at rising six since warmbloods were started in work much later than Thoroughbreds. He was a young horse with a little bit of mileage from what I could tell.

151

"I was in Germany in the fall, and know what horses are going for. He's a very nice horse with a great deal of potential but not this weekend. I would be misleading you if I told you otherwise, and I wouldn't be doing Kyffhäuser any favors."

We walked back to the barn and a stable hand was at the ready to take Kyffhäuser from us. Lockie removed his saddle, gave the horse another pat and the three of us walked outside.

"What should I do with this horse? Sell him?"

"Do you like him," I asked. "Personally like him? That's the reason you should have a horse."

Lockie opened the trunk and put his saddle inside.

Ed was stumped by the question. "I didn't buy him to ride him myself. I like the sport, the..."

"Social aspects," I supplied.

"Yes."

He was probably renting this farm in Florida because his friends were here for the winter. There was always one event or another scheduled in the horse world whether it was a show or a benefit gala. Equestrian sports were certainly more exciting, and more exclusive, than golf to some people.

The horses routinely traded hands in the same way fine art was auctioned off. People collected them and then deaccessioned them to get a newer, shinier model. That was the entertainment value of being part of the show world for some people, not the horses themselves.

That CB had been saved from such a fate made me very happy. And made him very happy, too. Now if he could only restrict his swishing to trail rides and leave the dance steps out of the workplace.

Like so many, Ed D'Angelis didn't take the time to know his horses and didn't think they had personalities. It was status, the current in-thing to do and gave him a full social calendar. What more could anyone ask for?

"This guy needs to be in a different program. He's not happy," I said.

"Horses have to be happy?" Ed asked.

"Yes," I replied.

"Let me send him to you and you can fix him."

I looked at Lockie.

"He doesn't need to be fixed," Lockie said. "You can't look at it that way. It's a process of discovery, of letting Kyffhäuser develop into the athlete he wants to be and can be. It's nothing that can be rushed. He got to this point because he was pushed every step of the way. That training has to be undone for him before he can make progress."

"Or I can just sell him."

"That's your choice. I'll be at the show tomorrow. You can think about it overnight. Tell me what you want to do," Lockie said opening the car door.

Ed nodded. "Fair enough."

We got in the car and headed up the driveway.

I turned to Lockie. "Do you really think that horse has potential?"

"Oh yeah."

13

AFTER AN EARLY BREAKFAST, Lockie and I hacked to the show grounds it was that close. It was a way to have a few minutes to ourselves but it turned out we weren't the only ones on the bridle path.

"It is beautiful here," I said, thinking how it was snowing back home according to last night's phone call from Greer.

"Napier is a community geared toward horses," Lockie replied. "You don't find many places like that anymore."

"Newbury used to be more like that but it changed."

"Would you like to live here?"

I didn't have to think about it. The weather right now was fantastic but it was all too grand for me. "No, but I am enjoying the visit."

"A year is a long time away but coming back for the winter circuit is a good business decision," Lockie said.

We wouldn't be able to afford the rental on a farm of the size Teche or even Ed D'Angelis had. A farm an hour or more to the northwest of Napier might be doable. I didn't want to be away from home for three months and certainly didn't want Lockie to be away. Maybe I would feel differently in a year. Things can change to an unbelievable degree in that amount of time.

"Do we need to know now?"

"If we want to rent a farm, probably," Lockie replied as we reached the showgrounds.

It was the largest equestrian facility I had ever seen and there were three rings with classes running simultaneously. New barns as big as aircraft hangers were off to one side and the parking lot in the distance looked like a holding area for a horse trailer factory. The main building was off to the left and by all the people headed in that direction, one might assume they were giving away flat screen televisions.

Counterpoint was fascinated, but not bothered, by all the activity, the flags flapping, the golf carts rolling past, the non-stop announcements over the loudspeakers as we tried to find the others from Acadiana South.

I brushed a stray fly off Counterpoint's neck. "You're the manager of the farm and if that's what you believe is the right thing to do, then it should be done."

"What is the downside?"

"We'll be separated for three months."

"Maybe you'll be tired of me by next winter," Lockie said reasonably.

As we found Tracy waiting for us at Teche's stable area, I turned to him. "Who says I'm not tired of you now?"

Lockie clutched his chest dramatically, then looked at his hand. "Am I bleeding?"

"You should be for suggesting such a thing." I slid off Counterpoint and Tracy took the reins from me and then from Lockie.

"You don't know," Lockie said seriously.

I looked around and there was no one who could overhear us. "You can get tired of your family but they're still your family."

"You think I'm your family?"

"You know that."

"Just say the word."

"Yes," I said. "Yes."

***

A half hour later I was standing ringside as the gate opened. Lockie entered on Counterpoint and they couldn't have looked sharper. His boots were polished to a high sheen, there wasn't a speck of dust on his coat, his gloves

157

were almost the same color as Counterpoint and the appearance was of a team with unlimited confidence.

This was not something I could get tired of. It was not how good he looked on a horse, it was that the essence of who Lockie was, was revealed when he was on a horse. He possessed great balletic elegance and a reservoir of sensitivity. There was never a time when his actions weren't calibrated toward kindness first above everything else.

As Counterpoint jumped the fences, never once did Lockie yank on his mouth. Counterpoint didn't raise his head, or rush and there was no scrambling even when galloping down the long lines. The round was smooth and flowing in the classical style. All that dressage training had paid off. When I checked the timer, they were ahead of the leader.

They finished with no faults in first position and the crowd erupted in applause.

I couldn't have been more proud of them both as he dismounted and Tracy was there with a cooler to throw over Counterpoint.

"How did it look?"

"It looked like the text book example of how to ride a jumper round," I replied.

"I think we could have done the triple combination a little better," Lockie replied looking back toward the arena.

"Why?"

"He chipped in to B."

"No, he didn't."

"You had to be on him to feel it."

"By how much was his stride off?" I asked.

"It could have been five inches."

"Or it could have been three."

"I don't think it was three. It might have been four."

"Lockie, please. It's not a Grand Prix class. Let's not measure in inches."

"These things are important," he replied.

"Nice round," Teche said as he came up to us. "I guess you wouldn't sell me that horse."

"He's not a good match for Acadiana," I replied.

"Why not?"

"He doesn't have a French name."

"*Contrepoint*," Teche said. "Sounds like French to me."

"He's Greer's horse and when these sisters latch onto something, they don't let go," Lockie replied.

"True dat," Teche said with a smile. "Just ride Roux as well."

"I'll try my best," Lockie said as Teche walked away laughing.

Twenty minutes later the jumper class was pinned and Lockie cantered Counterpoint around the arena for a victory lap. I felt a rise of pride when the announcer said "Counterpoint, ridden by Lockie Malone, owned by Bittersweet Farm."

Us, a little family farm in the northwest corner of Connecticut, taking a blue ribbon at the WEF. I had never imagined it happening nor imagined that I would care. That day I cared because it was important to Lockie. It was not an issue of ego but of excellence and accomplishment. Counterpoint was a product of our farm and our training program. That was worth having pride in.

Instead of me finding Lockie in the stable area, he found me by the rail, flipping through the program looking for his next class.

"Hi."

"If we were home," I started.

"Yes, we would," he said. "Did you call Greer?"

"No, I thought I would wait until after you ride Roux."

"Teche is having a buffet out on the cross country course. We can eat there, and afterward I'll ride Roux and the other horse Jennifer would have ridden." Lockie looked at the program, pointing to her name and the horse. "That should be around 4."

My eye was caught by a familiar name. "Nicole Boisvert. Greer's nemesis is here riding in the hunter ring. Let's go watch."

"I don't know what you think you'll see. Greer's a much better rider."

We walked toward ring 2, making our way through the crowds.

"Not according to the any judge who saw them ride in the same class."

"Nicole looks very good but she's not effective. Greer...I can't comment on what she looked like before I arrived at the farm. There was so much other stuff going on. Once Greer settled down, you know how proficient she is."

"If she had stayed here, would she have been able to win a jumper class?"

"She's certainly capable of it," Lockie replied as we found a spot on the rail to watch the hunters go.

"This was the class you were supposed to ride Kyff in," I said as I found the horse's name on the order to go list.

"He's scratched," Lockie replied.

I looked across the arena at the gate. "Don't count on it."

"Number 72, Kyffhäuser owned by D'Angelis Farm, ridden by Nicole Boisvert," the announcer said over the PA system.

Nicole trotted the large black horse into the ring and I braced myself. I didn't like the arch of his neck or how tight she was holding the reins.

"This should be fun," Lockie commented as Nicole made a circle and turned for the first fence, a plain panel.

A hunter should approach a fence at a calm, even pace. Kyff was fighting her every stride. He cleared the jump and tossed his head hard enough for the reins to slip through Nicole's hands.

"See. Pretty rider. Now she's in trouble."

Kyff immediately felt the pressure ease up on his mouth and he leaped forward as Nicole tried to gather the reins.

"Look at her seat. Her legs are loose."

It was all happening so fast, I found it hard to watch Kyff and Nicole at the same time. I really wanted to get the clues from his behavior and just wasn't as good at seeing it all.

Nicole managed to straighten him out to the fence. He over-jumped it and since she was perched on his neck, when he landed and bolted, it looked as though she hit her nose.

"That's gotta sting," Lockie said. "How about I go find Teche and see about lunch."

"No way!"

Leaning back, and pushing her feet forward, Nicole got Kyff to slow down for the third fence, a brush, and he took it reasonably well. She made the turn to the right to cross the arena on the diagonal and take an oxer. Then came the turn to the left and the two fences on the track.

Kyff didn't pay attention to Nicole at all and galloped over those jumps, and she managed to turn him for a birch log fence. When he landed, he bucked. She stayed with him, but he was in complete control. They made it over the next jump and the buck he threw on landing was breath-taking. It was a combo, fish-tailing to the left and then to the right.

Since Nicole's jumping position was essentially to lay on the horse's neck, she became a human lawn dart and hit the ground hard as Kyff raced around the ring squealing.

After twice around the outside, a couple members of the ground crew managed to flag him down and Kyff was caught.

Ed D'Angelis stepped up to us as his horse was lead from the ring. "I guess I should have listened to you."

"I guess," Lockie said.

"What can I say to persuade you to take him on?"

"Nothing. I don't work with people who refuse good advice. Come on, Tal, let's have lunch."

Ed followed us as we made our way around the arena. "What can I offer you? A bonus? A car?"

"I don't want to work with you," Lockie told him.

"Just sell him," I said. "He's not a horse you need."

"Isn't it true he's not worth much now?"

"Yes. He just lost about half his value by throwing a temper tantrum in public," I replied.

"It can't be a question of money," Lockie said as we made it to the stable area. "It's—"

"He doesn't want to be embarrassed in front of his friends," I said to Lockie.

He laughed. "That wasn't embarrassing?"

"Okay. You think I'm a jerk but you like the horse," Ed said.

"I do like Kyff, it's you who is the spoiler," Lockie replied.

A groom was walking the black gelding to cool him as we reached the D'Angelis stable area. I walked over and took the lead shank from the girl then stood in front of Kyff.

"What were you thinking?" I rubbed his forehead where his browband had been. "Do you have any idea how that looked?" I rubbed behind his ear, underneath the halter, and he lowered his head. "You could have hurt that girl. Are you ashamed of yourself at all? You should be. That was so naughty. Funny, but naughty."

Lockie came over to me. "We're going to lunch."

"What about Kyff?" I gave him a final pat.

"He's going to Bittersweet on the next van traveling north."

"What about Ed?" I handed the lead shank back to the groom.

"The only time we'll be aware of his existence is when the monthly check arrives."

"Cool. Greer will get along with Kyff just fine."

We headed to Teche's buffet.

"I was thinking the same thing."

∽ 14 ∾

TECHE WAS A VERY HAPPY MAN by dinnertime. His horses had placed first and second in the Crystal Citrus Classic with Cam on Tropizienne taking the blue and a nice sum of prize money which was going to my father to pay for Jetzt. Lockie took the red on Roux and left the money with Teche after an argument that lasted most of the evening. Bittersweet had received a ride on their van, and multiple rides on the jet as well as rooms at the estate. It wouldn't be right to keep the money. The argument in return was that we weren't taking up space Teche needed, and the little bit of food we ate was too picayune to mention as he pushed a bowl of bread pudding with brandy sauce at me.

It was an open house affair and nearly everyone at the show had been invited. Some came for drinks on their way to elsewhere, others nibbled at the extensive variety and number of amuse-bouches, and some stayed for dinner which, of course, came with several commercial interruptions by Teche for Chartier spices.

About mid-way through the evening, Ed D'Angelis appeared at the entrance.

"I'm going to go talk to Cam about tomorrow." Lockie began walking away.

"Oh thanks a lot."

"Hi Talia," Ed said, finding me in the crowd with the bowl of pudding. "Lockie's avoiding me."

"He's said all he needs to say. Then that's the end of it."

"He probably thinks I won't behave myself."

"Probably."

"What do you think?"

"It's a toss-up. There's as much chance that by spring you'll be trying to give us advice on what to do with Kyff as there is that you'll let us do the right thing by your horse. You seem like a meddler to me."

"You two do speak your minds, don't you?"

"Gee, Ed, there isn't that much time in life to play games and mislead people."

"In my world, obfuscation is the grease that keeps all the gears moving."

"That's not how I was raised."

"You had wise parents. I won't take up any more of your time but to say that Kyff will be on a horse transport tomorrow and should be in Connecticut by Monday morning."

"I'm glad about that. Thank you for making the right decision for him." I reached out to shake his hand.

"Just spell my name right when he starts winning ribbons."

"We'll do our best."

"That's what the last guy said."

"You might want to rethink saying something like that again to me in the future. Whoever the last guy was, and I don't care, Bittersweet Farm is different."

"I apologize. Good evening," Ed said without looking me in the eye and hurried away.

I found a flat, empty space on a table and set the uneaten bread pudding on it then walked outside. It had turned into a lovely evening, the kind we wouldn't see at home for months and I decided to visit Counterpoint.

My life had rarely made sense to me and now, after many months of stability, I realized that the ground had shifted beneath my feet again. Not in a bad way but it wasn't a change I had sought. This was a preview of my future. Bittersweet Farm and everyone there had gone into the horse business without awareness that it was happening.

Each new horse and each new rider had brought us closer to the point that tipped us into a new arena. The transformation must have begun when Butch went lame and Lockie found CB for me. I didn't want to show. I wanted a pet pony and CB was a 17 hand high one. Then Greer needed a new horse and the slide started in earnest.

Of course, ultimately, Lockie was responsible for the change. Without him, none of this would have happened. I probably would have continued attending The Briar School. Greer would still be friends with her now former friends. There would be no CB, no Counterpoint, no Ambassador of Good Cheer, no hunter pace, no Cam in our lives. I would be an okay equitation rider with not much knowledge of dressage or a horse that could do it and would be satisfied.

Now we had an expansive future that would undoubtedly offer me more surprises than I could handle. But it was the future I wanted because Lockie would be a part of it.

I found Counterpoint's stall, opened the door, went in, and put my arms around his neck.

"What's the matter, Silly?" Lockie asked from the aisle.

"Nothing. For once, nothing at all."

***

We spent the evening with Cam and Tracy on the patio behind the barn while the party continued at the house. In less than twenty-four hours I would be home.

It seemed as though Lockie's phone rang every twenty minutes with an offer to ride someone's horse the following day. He turned everyone down, not because of the experience with Kyff, but because there was a small museum in downtown Napier dedicated to the early years of Florida tourism and he thought I would enjoy visiting it. There was just enough time between his last morning class and his first afternoon class, if we went during the lunch break.

At ten, he stood up and said it was time for him to call it a day. Lockie went to his cottage and I went to my room where I called Greer and gave her all the latest news, including the pending arrival of Kyff. Greer told me about the Zuckerlumpens' progress striving for equitation perfection while she stood in the middle of the indoor freezing. "Heads up, heels down, don't rest your knuckles on your pony's neck." She threatened to make a recording of the instructions and simply put it on repeat. I agreed the girls had a short attention span and whatever was happening was all they could focus on. They were doing better than I had done at the same stage. I remembered being baffled and confused by every direction I was given,

After I had taken my shower and slid between the sheets, no electric blanket or down comforter required, Lockie called to say goodnight.

The next morning I was standing in the warm-up area watching Lockie and Cam work when my phone rang. It was a number from New York. I had to think who I could possibly know there, gave up and clicked it on.

"Talia, it's Ryan. You told me to call if I had a problem." She managed to get the words out in spite of crying at the same time.

"What's wrong and where are you?"

"I'm outside of Barn 1. It's where the Pitch Pine Farm horses are stabled."

"I'll be right there," I told her beginning to hurry in that direction.

"I just rode Ding in the pony hunter class. I don't know what we did wrong but when we got out Bill started shouting at me. He yanked my arm so hard, my feet left the ground!"

I was jogging, something I did not routinely do. "Who's Bill?"

Ryan was sobbing and couldn't speak for a moment so long it was painful. "Bill Moran, my trainer."

I could see the barn up ahead and wondered how this wasn't considered child abuse.

"I want to go home!"

Pushing my way through the crowd, I saw her sitting in the dirt outside the barn and sliding my phone into my pocket, ran up to her. "Ryan. It's okay. I'm here." I took one of her hands and helped her to her feet.

She threw her arms around me and cried.

"Who the hell are you?" A short man demanded as he exited the barn.

"Who the hell do you think you are?"

"I'm Bill Moran, Ryan's trainer."

I crouched down and pushed the hair out of Ryan's face. "Go get your pony, we'll give him a little walk to the warm-up area."

Ryan walked down the aisle.

"She has classes this afternoon and I expected her back here ready to work."

"Disabuse yourself of the idea that will ever happen again," I replied.

"You'll butt out of this if you know what's good for you." He took a step closer to me, threateningly.

"If you give me or Ryan one ounce more of trouble during this show, I'm calling the police."

His face turned bright red. "For what?"

"Child abuse. Child endangerment. I'll bet there are a list of charges and any one of them will put you in jail. Wait until her father finds out how you've been treating her."

"You're not going to tell him."

"I have no reason to protect you and all the reasons in the world to protect her from you."

Ryan led the pony to me and I put my hand on her shoulder.

"Put everything of hers in a tack trunk and have one of your grooms bring it to the office of the manager of the showgrounds."

Bill Moran nearly had steam coming out his ears. "You're giving me orders?"

"I said one more problem, didn't I?" I pulled the phone out of my pocket and began to key in 9-1-1.

"Okay, okay. Get the brat out of here."

"Apologize," I said.

"Sorry."

"Thank you," I replied. "I hope you have good luck with the rest of the show circuit."

Swearing under his breath, he went back into the barn.

"Want to ride?"

Ryan nodded and I boosted her onto Ding's back, then put my hand on her knee. "Are you okay?"

She nodded. "My arm hurts where he grabbed me." She pushed up the sleeve and I could see the red handprint on her fair skin.

I used my phone to take a couple photos and then we began the long trek back to the warm-up area.

"Did I get you in trouble?" Ryan asked.

"No."

"What are we going to do?"

"You should call your father and tell him what happened."

"He's on location."

"I'm sure he's very busy but you are worth more than a movie."

Sighing, she tried to wipe her nose on her shirt. "In theory."

"In real life. This is real life, Ryan."

We went to the edge of the warm up area. Cam and Lockie came over to me.

I spokesmodeled the pony and rider. "Look what followed me home. Can I keep them?"

Cam and Lockie shared a look.

"I heard someone say there's orange ice cream for lunch, maybe we can eat dessert first," Cam said to Ryan. "If you don't want any, I'll have your share."

"I want some," Ryan replied.

He helped her off Ding and they left to find Teche's chef.

"What's going on?" Lockie asked as he got off Counterpoint.

I took out my phone and held it out for him to see the photo of Ryan's arm.

"Who did that?"

"Her trainer, Bill Moran. She got out of the pony hunter class and he started verbally abusing her then grabbed her

173

arm and started swinging her around. I told him to bring her things to the office and if he gave me any trouble, I'd call the police."

"Again with the police?"

"I never called the police."

"Your sister did."

"Oh. Yeah. I forgot about that."

"So now we have a little girl and a really typey pony and no place to put them. Do we have a phone number for her parents?"

"They're divorced. The mother is in Paris. The father must be an actor or something, is on location, I have no idea where."

Lockie pulled Counterpoint's reins over the gelding's head and we began to walk to the stable area.

"You did the right thing. You probably made an enemy in the process."

"He seems mean."

"He is. He has a reputation for being a thug with the kids. But when a kid thinks they might become a champion, being called a *dummkopf* is probably worth it."

"You don't believe that."

"I don't but by later this afternoon, some twelve year old will step into Ryan's place. There won't even be a ripple."

"We have to do things differently," I said.

Lockie smiled at me. "We already are."

15

TECHE WAS DELIGHTED to have Ryan stay at his farm and made sure she was well taken care of. There was a spare stall for Ding and he seemed good with the change. A couple men from the Acadiana crew went to retrieve Ryan's trunk and her belongings from the tacky motel room on the other side of town. Nothing of what brought the pair to the farm was mentioned again.

That night there was a *fais do-do*, a Cajun dance party with a Zydeco band playing on the terrace and Teche danced up a storm with Ryan after showing her the steps. She was smiling and giggling as he twirled her around.

"I know her father," Cam said as we watched from the sidelines.

"How?" I asked.

"You do know he's a famous actor."

175

"No kidding," I said.

"Don't you two go to the movies?"

I shook my head. "I used to go with Rogers but only art films. I don't know anything about celebrities and whoever they are."

"Adam Saunders is a hot property now. He's a leading man."

"Okay. She is very pretty," I replied. "He's not much of a father, is he?"

"What do you want him to do? Stay home?"

Lockie was shaking his head at Cam.

"Yes."

"Then he wouldn't have a career," Cam replied. "My father wasn't always home when I was growing up and look how I turned out."

"Not a good argument," Lockie commented.

I laughed.

"He's sending her to a private school, he gave her a terrific pony, she's got the use of a jet."

"She doesn't have a father. She doesn't have a mother. The trainer roughed her up. He probably charged them for a suite at a resort, stuck her in the Mangrove Motel and pocketed the rest of the money. She's twelve and living as an unaccompanied minor. Ryan's raising herself."

"I'm used to kid actors growing up fast. I had to be responsible for myself a lot of the time and I swear my parents love me. Yes, it seems strange, but I do have some good qualities."

"So you're an expert at this. How do we help Ryan?" I asked.

"I'll talk to her father," Cam said. "She goes to school so that's not an issue. The only pressing problem is that she's now without a trainer. We'll try to find her someone else near the school and then they can take the pony to their stable."

"I love plans," I said.

"That's the ticket. Think positive," Lockie replied.

***

By mid-morning, I was acting as Ryan's trainer as she prepared for her pony hunter class. Tracy had helped organize her, finding the correct jodphurs, the bows for her braids, the bridle with the full cheek snaffle and the spare saddle pad. She was happy, Sideshow was happy and I seemed to be the only one wondering what was going to happen later in the day when Ryan and I flew back to New York.

Lockie came up alongside me. "Do you still want to go to the tourist museum?"

"Yes. Her class is in ten minutes, I should be done and able to leave right afterward. I owe her for the flight. Her father was very generous—"

"—If he even knew."

"Whether he did or not, I still got a ride, so it's no big deal to help her for the two classes today." I watched her canter around the area. "We need our own jet."

Lockie laughed. "We can barely afford the gas for the horse van."

He insisted that our corner of Bittersweet Farm should pay for itself and I agreed with him, but the operation had been paralyzed by Greer wanting to ride on the winter circuit and then coming home, leaving Lockie and her horse fifteen hundred miles away. It was impossible to run a business under those conditions. If Counterpoint continued to place and raise awareness of our operation back in Connecticut then this absence would be worth it sometime later in the year.

"And walk," I called to Ryan. "Okay. Next year we buy a jet."

"Try to watch my class," Lockie said as he began walking away.

"I will push people to the ground to get there," I called to him and could see him nod.

Although my experiences in Florida were completely different from Greer's, I understood how she could be disappointed in it because I certainly was. It wasn't relaxing.

I had come to be with Lockie and while I was in proximity to him, our only time alone would be at the Tourist Museum. And I was glad to have that little bit.

Ryan rode Ding over to me. "Is he your boyfriend?"

"He's my trainer, the manager of Bittersweet Farm."

"That's your story and you're sticking to it?"

"How old are you again?"

"Twelve. Everyone says I'm old for my years."

"That's what they said about me, too. Let me give you some advice. Be twelve for as long as you can be."

The announcer called her class and we headed to the ring for medium pony hunters under saddle, where a cavalry of ponies was filing into the arena.

I thought of my Zuckerlumpens back home who would not be out of place here among the little girls on their miniature Thoroughbreds, each one cuter than the next. At that moment, I vowed never to bring them here. It was fine to show locally, maybe even go to Pennsylvania but I would need one assistant per rider to make sure they weren't dragged across the showgrounds or painting hooves with purple glitter.

Such things had never occurred to me at their age. I had learned to braid manes and tails by practicing on Butch. I never thought to weave pink pompoms into the braids. Of course, if I had, Greer would have made me the laughingstock of New England. In a way, Greer had been good to me, keeping me from embarrassing myself unknowingly. Someday, when she could accept it, I would thank her.

The gate closed and all the riders tried to find a place on the rail, or a spot where they thought the judge could see them. I had advised Ryan to keep to herself, not to pay much attention to anyone else and remember that it was her job to show Ding off to the best advantage. This was not Bill Moran's philosophy of showing and he insisted all his students jockey for position even if it meant circling or cutting someone off. I told Ryan that the judge would find any rider doing exactly what was requested even if there were moments when other ponies blocked her from view. The arena was so large and the ponies so small, I believed that whole-heartedly. She didn't but followed my suggestion and rode through the entire class on the rail.

The ponies and riders left the ring, the judge made her decision and numbers were called to return. Ryan took the red and not surprisingly when I caught a glance at Bill Moran's face, it was nearly the same color.

She came out of the ring beaming and kissed Ding's nose.

"Beautifully ridden. You did a perfect job," I told her.

"There's room for improvement, though," she replied.

"We're all learning and growing, every single rider and horse on the showgrounds. Be happy he didn't throw a shoe while you were out there. I have to go watch Lockie. Tracy will take care of you, and see that you both have lunch."

180

"I sure will," Tracy replied throwing a cooler on the pony.

"Thanks, Talia," Ryan said.

"You're welcome," I replied, hurrying off to the jumper ring.

Lockie's class was already in progress and I found a small space next to Cam that I squeezed into.

"He didn't go yet, did he?"

"No."

"That's good."

"I'll work it out with Ryan's father and let you know. He's very angry about Bill Moran. I wouldn't be surprised if he didn't sic his lawyers on him."

"I wouldn't like to see that. It's just more upset for Ryan."

"If you're twelve thousand miles away, it's what you can do," Cam replied.

I sighed.

"My father does a lot of work outside the country, it's normal for me."

"But your mother is home."

"Yes. She's been based in New York for most of my life."

"You had someone."

"Everyone has something to deal with," Cam replied.

A bay horse was going over the fences. After bringing four rails down, I stopped counting.

"Ryan seems pretty well-adjusted to me."

"To you," I countered.

"How about to you? Your life was so normal?"

"No. Neither my life nor Greer's was close to normal. But at least I had a home. I lived at the farm and went to school only during the day."

"Who was there to greet you?"

I shook my head. "My father was in the city most of the time. Until Jules, it was a revolving door."

"I understand. You turned out okay. Greer turned out okay."

"Are you serious?"

Cam smiled. "Yeah, I am."

Lockie's name and number were called and were flashed on the jumbotron as he and Counterpoint entered the arena. They hand galloped for the first fence, a plain rail but on either side, there were huge representations of granola bars, a sponsor of the show. Counterpoint may have looked at them but he cleared the jump easily and went on to the next.

I thought of the saying "Those who can, do. Those who can't, teach." Lockie never asked us to do what he couldn't do, and sadly for us, he did everything much better than we could. He was more than good, he was a natural. Everything had come together to make him and outstanding rider. Maybe even his accident and the time off he had been forced to take, contributed to the depth with which he approached riding.

His abilities were not going unnoticed here. I heard the people behind me talking about him. I knew Lockie was getting many calls to ride other horses. Once I left, he would stop saying no. Why shouldn't he say yes? This was what he had worked toward for most of his life.

Dragged to lessons, dragged to shows, I was never willing, never had the intention of horses becoming my future. Of course I loved Butch, I loved being with him, but all the rest was Greer's métier. That I had absorbed anything from all that schooling was a shock to me. At least, I knew how not to teach.

Lockie had a clear round and the fastest time. It was no surprise that twenty minutes later he and Counterpoint had won the class. As soon as he exited from the arena, so many people converged on him that Cam and I couldn't get near him.

"Let him do this, Tal," Cam said.

I nodded.

***

At the Museum of Florida Tourist Gifts, we were confronted by a brown wooden tramp art orange on a pedestal.

"What's tramp art?" I asked the docent as she approached to greet the only two people she had seen in days.

"Tramp art was carved from pieces of discarded wood, usually cigar boxes. That's why there are many small pieces fit together to make the whole. This orange is very rare since it's round and most boxes are—"

"Rectangular," Lockie supplied.

The gray-haired woman's face lit up. "Exactly. You will see boxes, containers, picture frames, some of them very intricate, but to see something like our orange? Let's say we are extremely proud to have it."

"I can see why," I replied.

Lockie had changed into jeans and paddock boots for our trip to town so he might go unnoticed, as if he didn't walk and move like a horseman.

"Are you here for the horse show?" The woman asked.

"Yes."

"Everyone is. But they're too busy to visit us, and it's a niche museum. Have a look around and if you have any questions, I'll be at the desk of the gift shop. Nothing is made in China. They're all collectible items from the past. You'd be surprised at what we find in local antique shops."

"Interesting," I replied, thinking how little credence Victoria would give a postcard with a train heading south and a palm tree next to the track.

"Thank you," Lockie said and we entered the main room.

It was decorated as a living room, although I hoped no one ever lived like that. There was furniture upholstered in green and yellow palm frond fabric. On the coffee table, there was a box of Captain Alvarez cigars and a orange shaped ashtray. On the wall was a hand fan depicting a bouquet of orange blossoms.

In the next room, there were hundreds of framed orange crate labels on the walls. In display cases, there were orange salt and pepper shakers, orange jewelry boxes and a set of orange themed dinnerware.

"I think I've neglected to consume my share of oranges while here," Lockie said as we continued into the next room.

"You must rectify that," I said as we entered the flamingo room and cringed at the stunning pinkness of it.

Hurrying through, past the large flamingo floor lamps with pink shades, we reached the Everglades room and saw all manner of alligators—ridden, fought, led and worn. There was no lack of imagination when it came to what people could do with them, including stuffing them in a can so they could be ingested later.

The kitchen was replete with every tool and gadget known. The set of tools with handles shapes like palm trees, and bowls shaped like coconuts did nothing to outshine the sunflowers, orange blossoms and citrus fruits, not forgetting to mention tomatoes, strawberries and mangoes spilling out of everything from everywhere.

"Just imagine. Any one of these priceless treasures was purchased on a holiday to Miami Beach and brought home to Minnesota to stay in an attic for forty years until the call for tourist vintage gifts went out across the land and wound up here."

Time slipping away from us, we passed on going upstairs and stopped at the gift shop instead. It was practically a requirement, and I bought a large vintage citrus design platter for Jules. If she couldn't use it to serve lemon bars, I was sure there were other ways to make it a cherished item in our kitchen.

"Would you consider coming back and staying here for the rest of the WEF?" Lockie asked as we left the building and walked to the car.

This was not something I expected to hear from him. "Not just the weekends but all week?"

Lockie nodded.

"Why?"

He shrugged. "I miss you."

I stuttered for what seemed a very long while trying to find words to say what wasn't in my head. "You put me in charge of the barn."

"Greer can do it."

"She's working with Amanda on the Ambassador of Cheer project. We're taking the get-out-of-high-school-free

186

exam the first week of February. I promised the Zuckerlumpens we'd go to a show in a couple weeks." I stopped. "You are so much more important to me than any of these things, I don't want you to think that's not true. There isn't a moment in the day that I don't I miss you."

"No. I'm being selfish. Go home. Take care of everything I stuck you with."

I opened the car door. "If I come a few of the weekends, can you come home earlier?"

He raised his hands at me.

We both got into the car. "I know. This is for the farm. You can't come home on the weekends, what about—"

"During the week?"

"Yes. Leave Monday and come back on Thursday. How much...let Cam ride Counterpoint. He can ride fourteen horses a day and it doesn't bother him. Counterpoint doesn't need to be trained, just kept in training. Tracy can exercise him."

There was no way I could arrange a free weekend without impacting other people for almost a month.

Lockie was silent for a stretch. "We should meet in Virginia Beach where no one knows us. We'll get a room at the Seaview Motel and walk on the beach, pick up starfish and throw them back in the ocean."

There was something so wistful the way it was said, I knew there must be an underlying issue. "What's wrong?"

"I need a day off."

"Take it. Do you have a headache now?"

Lockie started the car and began driving back to the showgrounds.

"Where are your meds?"

"I have a class in two hours. I can't take anything."

"I am so calling Dr. Jarosz when I get home."

"Threats."

"If needed. What can we do now to help you?"

He didn't say anything.

"Lockie."

"If I lay down for a while, would you get Counterpoint ready and call me when there are ten riders before I have to go? Then I'll drive to the showgrounds and just get on and ride."

"Yes."

"I'll be fine."

"You should have your head examined," I replied.

"I did. It's cracked."

He dropped me off at the showgrounds and went on to Acadiana South. I found Cam who was riding in the first class after lunch but there were forty horses in front of him and Tabiche was just being brought onto the aisle.

"Ryan's looking for you. She has a fence class and then it's time to leave. Where's Lockie?"

"Laying down. The Museum of Tourist Gifts was fine but the pink flamingo room did him in."

Cam looked at me. "I have an admittedly atypical family but the Swopes give us a run for our money."

"What are you going to do about Greer?" I asked as he pulled on his boots.

"Nothing."

"You're giving up on her?"

"I didn't say that. She needs some time and doesn't need to be pushed."

"Are you going to keep your horses at Bittersweet?"

"Until you give me my pony, yes."

"Greer will never give you Remington back," I said.

"There's your answer." He pulled on the other boot. "Sloane Radclyffe came up to me during the lunch break. She's looking for someone to ride a couple horses for her in the spring."

The name was familiar. "Is she that rich girl?"

"Yes. The family has a farm in Pennsylvania."

Greer had shown me a magazine article about her. "The Fascinating Heiress? Is that her?"

"I don't know about that but they have a lot of money and she says she's impressed by my reputation."

"Huh."

"As a rider," Cam added.

"What's wrong with the rider she has?"

"He's not winning, is he?"

"Like I'm paying attention."

"It's a Grand Prix horse named Midnite Socialite."

"That's what they call her. The Scintillating Socialite! Does she name all the horses after herself? How weird is that?"

Cam shook his head. "Whatever she's called, if I go down to Chester County and do some riding for her, that will give your sister some time to remove the burr from her pan...from under her saddle."

"I hope you're right."

Ryan ran down the aisle. "Tali! Tali! My class is in twenty minutes!"

"Is Ding ready?" I asked.

"No!"

Tracy brought Cam's saddle out of the tack room. "Don't worry, Tal, I'll get him."

"Ryan, get your pony, pick out his hooves and brush him while Tracy helps Cam."

She looked at me.

"Don't you take care of your pony yourself?" I asked.

"Bill said we weren't smart enough."

"You just got a PhD in pony maintenance. Go get him, put him on some cross ties and get busy."

Ryan stood there, looking at me.

I looked back at her. "Three. Two. One. Why aren't you running to his stall?"

"I didn't think you were serious."

"If you're not going to do some of the work yourself, no one in this barn will help you. You're not going to help her, are you, Tracy?"

"Wouldn't dream of it." She tightened Tabiche's girth.

Ryan ran down the aisle to Ding's stall.

Cam laughed. "I'm not taking lessons from you."

"My sister is worse," I replied.

"No. Your sister is fierce and beautiful and sharper than the edge of a knife."

I thought Cam might have known her better than any of us did.

***

Ryan cantered Ding to the arena so that was her warm-up and she entered the ring before the gate was closed by a steward. Right then I made a decision that the Zuckerlumpens were responsible to get to the class in sufficient time. They would all wear watches and carry a list of their classes in their jacket pockets. I was not doing this again. I knew I would be doing something else, but this exact situation would be avoided. If they didn't make a class, that was unfortunate, but not my problem.

Butch and I had managed to make it to the in-gate in plenty of time at every show without someone functioning as my nanny. These kids could do it, too. It occurred to me that having one other person at a show to help me would not be enough. How did I do nearly everything by myself? I couldn't remember.

While waiting for all the ponies to go, I kept my eye on the time for Lockie. There was a little over an hour before his class would start and then nineteen horses before Counterpoint. It would go fast. Tracy would have Counterpoint ready to go, I would warm him up and then when Lockie arrived he could have time to prepare himself.

I hoped.

For the last four days, nothing had gone as planned.

Ryan entered the ring, made her circle, and took the low brush jump. The next fence was a panel following a right turn. She had made a left and was lost in a sea of standards and rails most of them facing her in the wrong direction.

The gate opened and Ryan rode out.

"I'm sorry," she said to me and gave Ding a pat.

"We have all done it. Help Tracy cool him down and get ready to go home. I have to get on Counterpoint."

"Can I watch Lockie ride?"

"You may if you finish all your chores. Your horse always comes first. There's no pawning him off on someone else. You make sure he is comfortable after his work-out or class."

Ryan looked at me as if this was a new idea.

"That's part of being a good horsewoman," I said.

It was obviously a concept Bill Moran had never mentioned to his students and I hoped Ryan's next trainer would have greater demands on her than just getting on and looking cute.

Tracy handed me Counterpoint's reins, gave me a helmet then a leg up and I walked him to the warm-up area. Lockie's class would start momentarily and the other riders were preparing as I joined them. I tried to find a corner off to one side where it was less crowded and we wouldn't be in anyone's way as they jumped back and forth over the couple fences.

Keeping an eye on my watch, and which numbers were leaving for the ring I could judge the progress of the class. I called Lockie on my cell phone and he told me he was already on the way.

Just like for Ryan, if he didn't make the class, it wasn't a life-altering event but five minutes later he appeared, dressed perfectly, looking rested and we switched places. I spotted him as he popped Counterpoint over the fences and then headed to the arena.

"Do you feel better?"

"Yes, Tal, thank you."

"What can we do—"

"Don't make a big deal of it."

"Is this why you wanted me to stay in Florida?"

"I told you why. I miss you."

Before leaving for the airport, I would ask Tracy to offer him more help, at least take some of responsibility for getting on Counterpoint and was sure that wouldn't be a problem. It was going to be harder since he was riding for Teche, too, but it could be done. Maybe Dr. Jarosz could help with his meds. Lockie didn't want to ride if he had taken something labeled "may cause dizziness" but there might be something else he could take in between the usual doses.

I felt I had let him down. I should have done this before he left the farm. Why I kept believing him when he said he got a clean bill of health must have been some kind of wishcasting on steroids. Of course, Lockie could have a good check-up and still have headaches for the rest of his life no matter how much effort we put into managing the pain. There wasn't necessarily a cause and effect, that he could avoid doing one thing or several and that would solve the problem. He accepted his limitations. I hadn't entirely.

Cam came up alongside of me and watched a blood bay mare go over the course.

"Don't worry about him."

"Cam—"

"I know. You can't help yourself. We live in the same cottage. It's not as though he has no one looking out for him."

"He doesn't know when he's over-doing it. Instead of taking a break, Lockie keeps going, and then gets worn-out. If you go that far, it's harder to come back."

"What I like about you two sisters is how deep your emotions go. You both care so much. How outsiders may perceive this behavior doesn't cross your minds at all."

"You're wrong about that. I know people think we're more than a little crazy, way out of control and several other assorted uncomplimentary terms."

"But it doesn't stop you."

"No," I admitted. "It doesn't even slow us down."

Cam smiled. "That's what makes you so unique."

"I don't see how. Lots of people act out."

"That's not what it is. You're both so passionate about doing the right thing. So few people know what that is anymore, but you do."

I thought about it for a moment. My mother would have been very pleased to hear that even if I did think Cam was exaggerating. "Do you really want Remington back?"

Cam laughed. "He's happy at Bittersweet."

Lockie and Counterpoint entered the arena and began a slow trot around the fences.

"He's such a quiet rider," Cam said. "I'm a power rider but Lockie uses both instinct and intelligence. It's a very unusual combination."

"What does the future hold for him?"

"I'm not Madame Fortuna but he had a name for himself after he aged out. Then he went into eventing and started at the bottom. He was working his way up when he had the accident. I think he'll make a name for himself again."

That's what concerned me. Not that Lockie would achieve what he should but that someday Bittersweet Farm, in a quiet little town in the northwest corner of Connecticut, would be too small for his talent.

Counterpoint began to gallop to the first fence and cleared it easily.

"I don't know if he's a better trainer or better rider," Cam said studying the round.

"Can't someone be both?"

"Perhaps. I'm a better rider."

"You've been wonderful training Greer. Part of what we're seeing is work you did with her and Counterpoint. Lockie didn't do that on his own."

Cam put his arm around my shoulder and gave me a squeeze. "You're very sweet."

"That may be but what I said is true."

Lockie and Counterpoint made the round look more composed and effortless than the other horses we had watched. The fences seemed incidental as they galloped over the course, paced beautiful, distances judged impeccably, rhythm found and maintained.

"That's the hours and hours of dressage. Counterpoint is in balance. He's supple, flexible and soft," Cam said as they jumped a liverpool. "People don't take the time to do what Lockie does. I don't take the time. I don't even know that much about dressage."

"Come home and learn," I replied. "It's part of the program."

"If Lockie places above me while we're here, I will."

There was rousing applause as Counterpoint cleared the last fence and took the number one position on the jumbotron leaderboard.

Lockie was dismounting and Tracy was throwing a cooler over Counterpoint when we reached them.

"Good job!" Cam said.

"It was beautiful," I said. "How do you feel?"

"I'm fine. You have to leave now, don't you?"

I nodded. Ryan had to get back to school and it was still a long flight even without being groped and x-rayed by the TSA.

"Call me when you get home, so I know you're alright," Lockie said.

"I will. Good luck on Roux. Try to come home."

"Try to come back."

Cam rolled his eyes.

"See you, Silly," Lockie said.

Less than an hour later, Ryan and I were in the air over Florida while Lockie and Cam prepared for their next class.

Greer was waiting for me and a driver was waiting for Ryan. I wished her luck on the rest of the Winter Equestrian Festival, waved goodbye and gave Greer a big hug.

"What's that for?"

"I missed you," I said and went around to the passenger side door of the truck.

"You were gone four days."

"Didn't you miss me?"

Greer started the engine. "I sure did. Those pony riders require full time oversight."

"Yes, they get into everything."

"Cute."

"Very."

Greer steered the truck onto the road heading home. "We were like that?"

"I don't think so."

"How is Lockie?"

"He had a headache this afternoon. I have to call the doctor tomorrow and see if there is something he can take while riding that won't make him dizzy."

"Try not to worry about him, it's not good for you either," Greer said. "How is my horse?"

"He won the class I watched before we left."

"How many horses were in there?"

"I think it was forty-seven."

Greer didn't reply, but she didn't need to. I could guess what she was thinking. "He's a better rider than almost everyone on the grounds, you can't compare yourself to him. Even..."

"Who?"

"Um."

"You can say his name."

I didn't want to fight with her all the way back to Connecticut. "Cam."

"Cam. So what did he have to say?"

"That Lockie is a very good rider." The less I said about him, the better it was.

"When is he moving his horses from the farm?" Greer asked.

"As soon as he reacquires Remington," I replied.

Greer didn't stop her tirade until we pulled up in front of our barn.

Nicely played, Cam, I thought as I got out of the truck and went to hug CB.

After a quick pass through the barn, we went up to the house where I was surprised to find my father waiting for me. "I thought you were in Texas.

He came over and wrapped his arms around me. "I came home to hear all about your winter break."

"You will not believe everything that happened," I said squeezing him tight.

***

Later that night, my phone rang.

"Hi. You know I'm okay. I called you the moment the wheels touched down in Poughkeepsie."

"But where are you now?"

"I'm on your side of the bed."

Neither of us said another word.

16

KYFF ARRIVED MID-MORNING and stepped off the gooseneck trailer looking more magnificent than when I saw him last. The transport had parked on the road because the rig was so long that it would be almost impossible to turn it around or back it out of our yard.

"He almost got away from us in North Carolina," one of the men said, handing the lead shank to me.

"What do you mean?" Greer asked.

"We take them off to walk around, stretch and pee. It has to be done on a long trip. And he just kept walking."

I looked Kyff in the eye. "What is your problem?"

"In Maryland, it took two of us to hold him. I thought I was hanging onto one of those cartoon blimps in the Macy Day Parade. Huh. He's all yours now."

The two men laughed and began lifting the ramp.

"Do you want help, Tal?" Greer called to me as she took our some bills to give to the men.

"If he runs, I'll let him go. He'll just get to the barn."

"And the house."

"Everyone has seen horses run by the windows," I replied.

"He runs across the ice on the pond and falls in. You explain that to the fire department when they come to rescue him."

I put my hand on his neck as we started to the barn. "You're not that stupid, are you."

Butch, Remington, Foxy and Garter practically turned themselves inside out to see the new horse walking toward their field. I didn't know why they were making such a fuss. New horses arrived all the time and there was never a welcoming committee with tails up, dashing back and forth on the fenceline.

I led Kyff into the main barn and clipped him to some cross ties so we could unwrap his legs in order to check him over.

"What's the deal with this horse?" Greer asked as she began unwrapping his near legs and I did the off side.

"He's upset."

"Why? Because no one he knows speaks German?"

"Maybe."

"Vhere are his papers?" Greer asked in as much of an East German border crossing guard accent as she could muster.

"We could get him a language learning course. How to speak English in twenty easy lessons."

"We could put him next to the Hanoverian Schtumpenyanken and they can relive their old beer garden days."

"What is CB?"

"The kind of horse they use to pull stumps out of the ground."

I laughed. "You are so awful."

"But funny."

"Very."

A felt a warm breath on the back of my neck as Kyff dipped his head to reach me. Or bite me. With his reputation, it was hard to know.

I gave his leg a pat and stood.

"What are we supposed to do with him?" Greer asked.

"He's being layed up until Lockie comes back from Florida."

"That's a long time to stand around doing nothing."

I pulled a piece of carrot out of my pocket and offered it to him. He didn't take it. I broke it in two smaller pieces. He didn't seem to understand. I pushed a piece in his mouth and he let it fall out. I pushed another piece in and held his mouth shut.

"Have you ever seen a horse who didn't know what a carrot was?" I asked.

"Break them up into his lunch then he'll associate the taste with the smell. These upper tier show horses are treated like battery chickens."

I pictured the rabbit with the drum. "What's that?"

"Not battery like electricity. Buildings filled with stacks of cages in England for laying hens. Commercial production."

I didn't pay nearly enough attention to the Grand Prix show circuit because this was the kind of thing I didn't want to know.

"I was in the stable area at Gatcombe one year and I overheard a rider say 'I thought he was a machine and was surprised to find out he was a horse'."

"Did you yell at him?" I asked.

"I wanted to. I was only eleven."

I unbuckled the front closure of his blanket. "We better put another blanket on him, don't you think?"

"Definitely."

"Lockie and I talked a little about the direction Bittersweet Farm was taking," I said. "We don't think we should be like everyone else. Bittersweet's never been about that. Besides, we can't find batteries big enough to fit in Kyff's back."

He spit out the carrot.

***

"What do you want me to do with Kyff?"

It was almost ten before Lockie called from his cottage. Cam was out with some other riders at a bar in Napier but a live band playing in a small space with people laughing and drinking was hardly a choice Lockie would make, knowing the consequences and knowing he had horses to ride in the morning.

"What do you want to do with him?" Lockie asked.

"I don't know," I replied.

"No one does or his problem would be solved by now."

"I don't have the experience you do."

"No, you don't but I didn't acquire it by magic, I learned by doing. Sometimes it was a suggestion someone gave me, other times it was trial and error. I keep trying different techniques until one of them worked. Then I refined it until I understood why that attempt worked."

"So make a suggestion."

"You tell me what you're going to do with him. You can do it, Tal."

"I don't want to do the wrong thing."

"I would never worry about that when you are involved. What's your impression of Kyff?"

I thought for a moment. "The two men who drove him here had problems handling him. I walked him down the driveway with a loose lead shank. Greer and I removed his shipping boots, put another blanket on him, then stuck him in the stall next to Jetzt so they could speak German to each other. We didn't have any trouble with him."

"Tomorrow, what are you going to do with him?" Lockie asked.

"Turn him out."

"Ride him."

"No, I don't think so. He's not ready."

We discussed Kyff for the next hour and by the time we said goodnight, I had a plan.

***

The next morning after their breakfast, I turned Kyff out with Butch and the ponies. Everyone went nuts and galloped to the crest of the hill, snorting and kicking out. I made a mental note to have Kyff's shoes pulled. He could go barefoot for the next month and it wouldn't hurt him at all. It wouldn't hurt anyone else either.

When I reached the house for my own breakfast, the mood was decidedly morose at the kitchen table. I hung up my jacket and left the barn boots by the door.

First choice. "Who died?"

"If only it worked like that," Greer replied.

Second choice. "What did Victoria do now?"

"She just hit some kind of milestone in sales. Everyone is talking about her."

"Fine. What does that have to do with us?"

"Stop making sense," Jules said to me.

"She wants to be interviewed in the carriage house because one of the networks is going to drive here from the city," my father explained.

"The condo isn't cute enough," Greer finished.

"Well, no," I replied, sitting at the table. "She may not use Lockie's house again. What's for breakfast?"

I was reaching for a morning bun when the door flew open.

"Hi, lovelies!" Victoria called out to us.

"Shut up," Greer replied under her breath.

"I heard that, darling!" She unwrapped a scarf from around her neck. "Hello, Andrew, dear."

Greer made a choking sound.

Victoria hurried to the table, pretending to be chilled to the bone. "Jewel, could I beg you for a cup of coffee?"

"It's Jules," I said.

"Yes, of course it is," Victoria replied.

"The coffee maker is on the counter," my father replied. "We serve ourselves."

Victoria looked at him in feigned shock. Or perhaps it was real.

"This isn't an episode of *Newbury Abbey*." Greer picked up her plate and mug and brought them to the sink. "There are no upstairs maids, downstairs maids or waitresses to serve you."

"Please continue and I'll take notes. Maybe that can be my next book. It is rather a fascinating idea, isn't it? The young scion falls in love with the downstairs maid but he must marry the chaste daughter of Lord...Basingstoke. The downstairs maid is not virginal in the least and schools him in the finer arts Oxford neglected to provide. This is good."

"Shut. Up." Greer said as she pulled on her jacket. "Why did you drive out here?"

"I want to make arrangements to use the carriage house."

"No," I replied, finishing my tea. "You're not using Lockie or his house. Thank you for decorating it attractively but it's his home and not your showroom. Find someplace else."

"Andrew. You allow the girls speak to me like this?"

"They're not girls, they're young women and they can say and do whatever they see fit," my father replied.

Jules didn't look up from her fruit compote.

"Call Teche." Greer opened the door. "If you promise to mention his Hotter Than Hell spice mix three times, he'll be glad to have you park your butt on his loveseat for twenty minutes." She left the kitchen and closed the door.

I jumped up to catch her before she got too far. "Thanks, Jules." I stuffed my feet into my barn boots and went out the door, jacket in hand.

Greer was almost at the end of the path to the driveway.

"Wait up," I called.

She stopped.

"I had an idea. Instead of riding CB, I'll ride Wing."

"When?"

"To practice."

"Is everyone around me insane?" She asked. "Why?"

"Because CB doesn't need to practice and I do. Would you spot for me?"

"Yes."

"Then we'll take CB and Kyff on a trail ride."

"Who's riding Kyff?"

"You are."

"No. I don't want to commit suicide by horse."

"What are you talking about?" I asked. "Kyff's sweet."

"He bucked Nicole off."

"She was loose."

"Nicole!"

Greer's nemesis for the final three years of her equitation career, Nicole Boisvert was a sure thing. There was little point in holding the class when she was entered. Just have the steward open the gate, have her walk into the middle of the ring, and give her the ribbon and trophy.

"She's not that good, Greer. The judges just liked her. They were predisposed toward her instead of you. That's all it was. It's not like a real thing where you're judged on your ability. It's opinion, preference—"

"I never pinned over her."

"Don't exaggerate. You did and it's in the past. You..." I caught myself before mentioning the fact that she had pinned in Florida in a very large class. There was no point reminding her of Cam. "You're a very good rider with a very good trainer."

Greer sighed.

"If you want to take Wing on the trail and I'll ride Kyff, that's fine with me."

We walked into the barn.

"I saw Lockie ride Kyff."

"Lockie!"

"Lockie is really good but he's not endowed with superhuman ability. Kyff didn't misbehave. Well, there was one buck with him and I don't think..." I stopped.

"What?"

"Could it be that easy?" I asked.

"What, Talia?" Greer asked.

"I think I have him figured out."

"Are you going to share with me or not?"

I went to the tack room for my saddle and a bridle. "Tack up someone, we'll do this now and see what happens."

17

KYFF WAS BROUGHT ONTO THE AISLE where I put my saddle on him and a quartersheet over his back. He rejected the offer of a cookie. I held it up to his nose so he could get a whiff of the appley goodness. I waved it in front of his face so he could see what I was doing. I stuck an edge into my mouth and crunched down on it. It might have been appley good but it was also as hard as a rock.

"Hmm hmm hmm." I made a big production of liking the cookie and had his unwavering attention.

I held it up to his nose again, then chewed on it a little more. "Yum." I offered it to him, then when he reached for it I turned away. "No. You didn't want it before, why should you have it now?"

He took a step closer to me, pushing his nose at me.

"You're not convincing," I said. "Why do you deserve this very good cookie?" I chewed another edge deciding it would be necessary to get the vet over here and have my teeth floated if I went much further.

I wafted it past his nose again to keep his undivided attention then gave the cookie to Keynote who didn't need it but was a useful accomplice.

"That's too bad, Kyff. You missed out on the cookie." I made a big production of patting my pockets. "Here's another one! YUM!" I put it up to my mouth and Kyff put his nose in my face. "Do you want this? Are you sure? If you spit it out, you're not getting another one."

I held out the cookie to him on my palm. He nosed around with it, closed his lips around it and began to chew.

"What a good boy!" I gave him several pats on the neck and felt so bad that he had reached this age and never had a treat before. "Wow. Fantastic. Genius." I stopped for a moment and thought. "Didn't anyone ever give a damn about you?"

"Don't bury your head on his neck and start crying," Greer said as she led Citabria past us.

"Why not?"

"It doesn't help. Do something instead."

After unclipping the cross ties, I led him outside to the mounting block. Greer was already on Citabria who was seemingly unable to stand in one place. Kyff stood, waiting for me to settle into the saddle and then moved off.

"Hey, I didn't say to walk." I tightened the reins and he stopped. "Good boy!" I closed my legs and eased up on the reins and Kyff walked forward.

"Can we go now?" Greer asked. "With the wind chill, we'll be lucky if we don't turn into grim equine ice sculptures before we get back."

"You can turn back any time. Kyff seems decent," I replied as we caught up to her.

The wind was blowing light snow into our faces, and Citabria was less than pleased.

"When was the last time you took Citabria out?"

"I rode him yesterday. In the indoor. It's the middle of winter, Tal. If you haven't noticed, it's freezing. And now it's snowing."

"You can't just ride inside," I replied, as we turned into the field, snow up to the horses' knees. "It's unbalanced training."

"You always preferred hacking," Greer said.

"That's true!" I gave Kyff a pat on the neck and remembered the trouble Greer had at the state park getting Counterpoint to cross the river. "We'll go out together more often. I like company."

"You don't. You like being alone."

That was also true. I learned to like being alone and it still seemed comfortable and normal but being with someone was very pleasant, too.

"Do you want to trot up the hill?" I asked.

"What if he gets away from you? Bucks you off?"

"There's foot of snow. I'll never have a softer landing than this. I'm game."

"Okay."

A moment later, Greer and Citabria were trotting up the hill and I eased up on the reins so Kyff could follow.

"I'm counting on you, Mr. Kyff, to be a gentleman."

One ear rotated back to hear me.

"Yeah, well, do it. I know you can."

At that moment, Citabria began leaping up the hill. It wasn't a canter, it wasn't a gallop and it sure wasn't the trot it was supposed to be.

Urging Kyff into a canter in order to move in front of Citabria who looked like he was feeling just a little too good for my liking, then I reined back. Both horses trotted then walked.

"Good boy, Kyff!" I said and leaned over to offer him a piece of carrot I always had in my pocket.

He still didn't know what to do with it.

***

The family went out for dinner to an Italian restaurant, and while it was pleasant, I missed Lockie. Literally had missed him all afternoon.

214

I called him after getting off Kyff. Called him after getting off Wing, and called him after giving the Zuckerlumpens their lesson. All the calls had gone to voicemail, making me feel that I should have called Cam.

We had dessert but it wasn't as good as what Jules would do.

"Why did we come to an Italian restaurant when you're more proficient than they are?" I pushed my tasteless *zuppe inglese* away from me.

"Because, Dolcezza, this chef has received good reviews and I wanted to see if they were deserved," Jules replied.

Greer raised her hand. "I vote no."

I raised my hand. "Ditto."

We looked at my father who nodded in agreement.

"Next time we'll find a German restaurant," Jules said.

I'd never heard of one around Newbury but maybe I didn't leave the farm often enough.

***

After returning home, we all watched television for a while, then lost interest and went our own ways. I got in my truck and drove to the carriage house. It was starting to feel like home to me and I felt closer to him there.

My phone rang while I was reading in bed. The New York number, I never recognized.

215

"Hello."

"Hi Talia, it's Ryan."

When was I going to remember this? But in my own defense, I never expected to hear from her again.

"May I come for a training session tomorrow because I have to go to Florida and we haven't found a coach for me yet."

I tried to think who she could ride. Calling All Comets was just starting to get back into light work but he wasn't ready to do a serious forty-five minutes. It would have to be a horse and they were all so big for someone her size.

"Please, Talia. Everyone is in Florida."

"Okay. I'll figure it out."

Tyr. He was big but a cupcake. Uncomplicated and tolerant, he would be perfect for Ryan.

"Thank you. If I get out of school at lunch, I can be there by two. Is that good?"

"Sure."

The Zuckerlumpens usually arrived around three.

"See you then," Ryan said. "Bye."

"Bye."

Her father really had to take ten minutes away from his soon to be a major motion picture and attend to his child. This wasn't anyone else's responsibility. Didn't she have a nanny or a guardian? Wasn't there anyone to look out for her. Probably a lawyer was her go-to functionary.

I was happy to let her come here and ride, but there was no one for her in Florida and that's where she really needed some help.

My phone rang and I hoped it wasn't her, again, thinking of something else. Checking it, I saw it was Lockie.

"Hi."

"Hi. My battery went bad, so I got a new one on the way to Ocala."

"What were you doing there?"

"Cam and I were looking at horses."

"How are you?"

"I'm fine. How are you?"

"I want you to do me a favor."

"All right. What?"

"Buy Kyff."

"Why would I do that, besides that you asked me to? The farm can't afford him and we can't go to your father and ask for another loan. The farm has to pay for itself."

"You're a horse trader," I said. "Do your thing."

"Silly—"

"I got him figured out."

"That's several days less than I thought it would take you," Lockie replied. "Why do you want this horse?"

"I don't want him for me, I want him for you."

217

∽ 18 ∽

THAT WASN'T STRICTLY TRUE. I wanted Kyff at the farm. He deserved a chance at a normal life where he would be coddled, and given a Bock beer when I could legally buy beer. He was intriguing, handsome, and deserved to be understood. Whatever was going on with him was the result of bad training, it wasn't his personality.

My mother had always told me to try to assess people favorably first and let them prove whether they deserved a positive response or not. I was certain that extended to horses and dogs who didn't have ulterior motives the way people might. Kyff just wanted to be treated well. CB just wanted to be my pet pony. All the horses at the farm wanted a pleasant life. They wanted to comprehend what was being asked of them and given patience and respect.

We couldn't collect horses and not every horse that arrived at the farm could stay, but I felt that it was imperative that Kyff remain with us. I didn't want to run the risk that Ed D'Angelis would change his mind or lose interest in the horse world and sell Kyff out from under us.

Whatever Kyff had done, I trusted him to a far greater degree than his current owner. Ed D'Angelis needed to be permanently out of our lives.

With that thought persistently at the front of my mind, I tacked Wingspread, led him to the mounting block and got on. In the indoor, I forced myself to concentrate and rode the dressage test over and over again. Finding myself at K and having no idea what came next was not an experience I wanted to have in public.

"How many times are you going to ride it?" Greer asked.

"Until I'm sure of myself," I replied.

"When will that be?"

"Next year?"

"Talia. Give it a rest, please. It's training level. CB's so far beyond that it's laughable."

"I'm not!"

"What are you worried about?"

"I forget the tests all the time. Lockie has to stand there and tell me what comes next."

"You never forgot a course," Greer said. "We showed for years and your memory was perfect. This is not more difficult."

219

"CB is so good. What if I volte at the wrong letter?"

"What if he does one of his Lindy Hop moves?"

"That won't be my fault."

"You'll find a way to make it your fault," Greer replied.

That stopped me. She was right.

"Go and have fun or don't go but don't make yourself miserable." Greer turned and began walking out of the arena then stopped. "Life is too short, right?"

"Yes."

***

After the incident in Florida where she had made the wrong turn in the hunter class, I had Ryan practice courses on Tyr but she couldn't remember anything but a simple eggroll. Motioning her to the center of the ring, we stood there looking at each other for a while.

"Is your memory always this poor or is something bothering you?" I asked.

She studied Tyr's mane, then the rafters, then the stitching on her gloves. "My father is really angry with Bill Moran."

"Is he taking him to court?"

"I don't know. I don't want to be in trouble for saying anything. I don't want you to be in trouble for helping me."

"You're not in trouble," I said.

Ryan began crying and I went to her.

"If you don't want to go to Florida, don't go."

"I can't leave Ding there by himself."

"He's at a lovely stable being cared for by Tracy. He's fine."

"If I bring him home, I have no stable for him. He lived with Bill."

"Give me your father's phone number and I'll call him."

Ryan handed me her phone. "It's on speed dial. Number 1."

I pressed the button and waited until it was answered

"Hi, Ryan. I'm really busy right now, let me call you back," Adam Saunders said.

"Hi, Mr. Saunders. It's not Ryan, it's Talia Margolin and you should make five minutes to talk to me."

"What's this about?"

I moved the phone away. "Ryan, take Tyr to the barn and have Cap help you with him. Okay? Can you do that?"

She nodded and began to walk out of the building.

"Ryan doesn't want to go back to Florida and there's no one there to take care of her. She's concerned about the repercussions now that you're starting legal proceedings again Bill Moran. She's twelve. Where is her adult?"

"I'm making a movie that's budgeted at over a hundred million dollars. Send her back to school if she has nowhere to go." His annoyance was obvious.

221

Idiot. "Where does she live when she's not in school?"

"I have an apartment in New York and a house in Malibu. I hire a nanny. Okay? There's no point in having a nanny now when she's in school."

Pinhead. "Who was taking care of her in Florida?"

"Bill Moran."

"He put her in a cheesy motel room where there was no room service, no staff, no security. Why am I more concerned about your daughter's welfare than you seem to be?"

"That's the end of this Florida junket. Have the car bring her back to the school and she'll stay there until I finish this shoot. I hope that meets with your approval. Can I get back to the set now?"

"What about her pony?"

"Leave it in Florida. I don't care!" The famous movie star hung up on me.

***

"I think we just acquired another pony," I said entering the house to see Greer and Jules at the kitchen table having tea and almond shortbread cookies. "The movie star just told me to leave Sideshow Ding in Florida, that he didn't care what happened to it. Her beloved pony!"

"Do whatever you have to do make this right and charge him double for it," Jules replied.

"If he doesn't authorize our efforts in his daughter's behalf, can't he just refuse to pay?" Greer asked sensibly.

"You can give him so much bad publicity as a lousy father that he wouldn't dream of stiffing you," Jules said. "Send the bill to his accountant."

"Who's that?" I sat down for my tea and cookie before hurrying back to the Zuckerlumpens.

"Ryan will know. She probably sends her bills there already."

***

I was in the middle of the arena watching Gincy and Poppy try to trot over cavellettis without using their stirrups.

"I can't do this!" Gincy said, holding on to Beau's mane as she reached the end of the six-pole line.

The weather was miserable and it snowed a little almost every day. It never seemed to warm up past freezing and I had begun wearing chaps because they kept me warm as while standing in the dead cold of the indoor. Hat hair was my standard hairstyle because if I didn't wear a ski cap, I couldn't feel my ears by the end of the afternoon. No gloves kept my fingers both warm and flexible. Either I had robot hands or frozen ones.

"You have these things called legs. Inside legs are bones and what else?" I replied. There was silence. "Anyone?"

"Muscles," Poppy answered.

"Yes. That's what they are. Muscles!"

"Use them?" Poppy asked.

"Hey, that could work!"

Neither of the girls were strong enough and that was a shame but they wouldn't get stronger if they didn't work harder. The last thing I wanted to see was either girl jumping fences at the show and being dislodged from the saddle each time the pony landed. Nicole was loose and she fell off. Jennifer was loose and she fell off. Knowing what could happen, I wanted my riders stuck to their saddles.

We gave the line two more tries, then I allowed them to pick up their irons and go over it twice more. Both riders did well and ended on a positive note so I released them for the day.

They weren't lacking ability, they had lacked good training. It was so easy to sit on a pony and look cute. That posed picture style even passed as successful with some coaches but I wanted more for Poppy and Gincy. I wanted for them what Greer and I hadn't received until Lockie had arrived—an equestrian education.

When I went to the new barn with the girls, I found Greer with Amanda in the office working on the

Ambassador of Good Cheer project. It had been an assignment for me that ended when the year did. For Greer, it had become an integral part of her day. Amanda was giving her an advanced course on charities that went far beyond the one we had tinkered together for our final semester of high school. This was what Greer wanted to do and had enthusiastic support from our father and grandparents. I hoped that if Oliver stopped being a ham, or the program no longer interested people in the way it had, that Greer wouldn't feel she had failed. It was possible that the project could just run its course, she had a portable learning experience and it was time to move on to bigger challenges.

Greer waved to me and I went in. She held up a letter. "This is from a 4-H Club in Bethany. They want to know how to start an Ambassador of Good Cheer there!"

I think it was the first time I had ever seen Amanda smile.

***

Cap, Freddi and Greer decided to go to a newly released movie about a dollar store horse. That's what I called them. Someone who knows nothing about horses finds a horse hanging out, freebie-like, takes it home and in record time is winning fill-in-the-blank kind of championships on it.

This sort of movie generally had a very unpleasant turn of events for the horse, which always left me wondering why it wasn't the human run over by the snowplow. Cap insisted she didn't go to see movies like that and still hadn't seen *Sarge* for fear the horse was hurt in the story. If she wanted to take the risk with this movie, it was up to her, but I didn't want to be in the theater when Greer over-reacted to the predictably included horse-suffering scene.

My phone rang as I was sitting on the couch reading a book in front of the fire.

"Hi," I said.

"Hi, back. Kyff is almost yours."

"What does that mean?"

"He belongs to Cam right now," Lockie said. "Someone owed Cam, so he called in the favor, and we used that horse to trade for Kyff. How do you feel about that solution?"

"Better. Thank you. What is the price differential between Jetzt and Kyff?"

"You mean, can we trade Jetzt for Kyff?"

"Yes. How much more does Cam owe on Jetzt? We're not really talking money."

"We're not but your father did pay real money for the horse."

"What difference does it make if we have a fantastic horse and trade him for another fantastic horse?"

"Ask Amanda for some remedial math work," Lockie suggested. "We bought Jetzt to sell, not to keep. We need the money we were getting from the sale of Jetzt to Cam. If we trade with Cam for Kyff, then I'm assuming you think it's a one for one arrangement, no more money needs to change hands."

"Well, yes, that's what I was thinking. It was an even trade for the other horse to Ed D'Angelis, right?"

"Yes."

"And that proves that the value of a horse is what you think it is."

"How do you figure that?" Lockie asked.

"Because the moment Kyff threw those bucks in Napier, Ed said he lost half his value, so you just traded him, I'm assuming, a horse who performs well but is worth a lot less than Ed paid for Kyff."

"The pathetic part of this is I actually do understand what you're saying," Lockie replied.

"So you agree with me."

"No, I don't. It's terrible business."

"Lockie."

"Let me state this very clearly for you. Be serious here for a short amount of time. The money cannot come out of your father's pocket. The rest of the money Cam owes to Bittersweet Farm can't be ignored and we must pay your father back."

"You're not that kind of boy, I get it."

"You're not that kind of girl, that's what I like about you."

"Tell me what else you like about me."

"That you wanted to save this horse."

***

The night before the show, I slept for about twenty minutes, reliving every horse show that had gone wrong for me. At two, Greer came in, gave me Joly and turned off the light. She threatened to lose patience with me if I didn't knock it off and go to sleep.

It was dark when I woke, pulled on some clothes and took Joly out for his morning constitutional which included a visit to the barn where we discovered CB sleeping on the floor getting shavings all through his tail. Since we had hitched Lockie's trailer to his truck the previous afternoon, it was no secret that we were planning on going somewhere but Cap respected my mounting anxiety and didn't question me.

After breakfast, I walked CB up the ramp, Greer fastened the tail bar, and I went around back to help her lift the ramp.

"Ready?"

"No."

"Get in," Greer said and went to the driver's side.

"Maybe we should scratch because it's going to snow and the roads will be slippery."

"Did I do this to you?" Greer asked as she turned the rig onto the road.

"I did this all by myself."

"Were you always like this?"

"Yes."

"It must have been hell for you."

"Yes, it was."

"I'm sorry. I wasn't enjoying it either," Greer replied.

"What?"

Greer drove through the center of town, which was barely awake at that hour and took the left heading west.

"What was to like? Nicole was pinning over me in every class. No matter what I did, I couldn't please anyone and you were so..."

"I'm getting the blame for something?"

"You were so above it."

"How did you work that out?"

"You can have an air of disdain about you. That something is not worth your effort. There I was trying so hard at the only thing I could do and you were ever-present to remind me that it was futile and worthless."

"I'm so sorry. That wasn't disdain. Maybe a little. It was more acute discomfort that I was trying to hold in."

"I know that now. I said we were both screwed up."

"Less as time goes along," I replied.

Greer nodded and drove to Kohanza Farm.

Unsurprisingly, we were not the first trailer to arrive. The parking area was nearly full and Greer told the assistant we would be gone before lunchtime so he directed us to a spot where we wouldn't have trouble leaving. There was snow everywhere, even though, like we had, used the bucket on the tractor to try to move it elsewhere.

Greer parked and didn't get out. "Talia. I have to say something. I'm sorry about all the other shows, you're sorry, too, right?"

"Yes."

"This is a new beginning for you. You've got that great horse–"

"You said he was a Schtumpenyanken!"

"We can hitch Citabria in tandem with CB and they'll pull stumps together. He's a wonderful horse, and, for some reason, you can ride him and I can't. As if that makes sense!"

I laughed.

Greer smiled. "See. Make the best of what's not a very bad situation. You can do this."

We climbed out of the truck and while I got CB ready, Greer went to the show secretary to get my number. I had him tacked and with a wool cooler over him when I rested my forehead on his. "The worst that can happen is that I'll say we got lost and thought this was an audition for *Dancing With the Stars*. I'll do my best not to embarrass you."

I offered him a cookie, and unlike Kyff, CB, knew exactly what to do with it.

"I don't know why I'm here," I said to him. "It seemed like a good idea."

"It was a good idea," Greer said coming up behind me, pushing the number into my hands. "Your test is in ten minutes."

"Why? It's supposed to be at ten. It says on the prize list ten a.m." I pulled it out of my jacket pocket and held it up to her, pointing at the line.

"Well, cupcake, the class is running now." Greer whipped the cooler off CB and tossed it onto the trailer divider. "Get your helmet. Geez!" She reached for CB's reins as I ran back to the truck.

"The warm-up area, and may I say that's a misnomer since it's not even above freezing and the ring is outside, is to the right of their indoor."

She gave me a leg up and I settled into the dressage saddle.

"Go! I'll be right there."

I jogged CB toward the indoor and found the ring where there were already a number of horses trotting around. We began our own warm-up, trotting, then cantering, then circling, doing a shoulder-in, a haunches-in, a half-pass.

Greer waved to me. "Your turn and may I say you are absolutely nuts."

I walked CB out of the ring as she threw the cooler over us as best she could. "Why?"

"You have no idea how good you are. You're going to go in there and kill the test."

My name and number were called and I urged CB forward into the arena. Taking a deep breath, I tried to remember everything Lockie told me and everything CB told me. Then we began the test.

I was on autopilot having done the test so many times in the last two weeks. Working trot, circle left, working canter, half circle, get deep into the corners, transition at the letters, walk, working trot, canter, was that a swish, no, half circle, working trot. Down the centerline. Halt. Square. Salute. Breathe.

We left the indoor and I slid onto the ground as Greer threw the cooler over CB then gave me a hug.

"That was perfect! You should have heard people whispering about you. And no, it wasn't about how horrible it was. That guy over there, no, don't look, tall guy in the field boots, look now. He said you were the best new team he's ever seen."

"Who is he?" I whispered to her.

"No clue," she whispered back.

"That's Armand Saller," a woman next to us said with a smile. "I couldn't help overhearing. He's a quite well-respected dressage rider and I agree. You did do very well." She gave CB a pat on the neck. "Who is this?"

"Freudigen Geist," I replied.

"He is a very handsome and talented young man."

"CB's her pet pony," Greer assured her, taking the reins from me. "He just wants to sit in her lap."

"He's a little big for that," the woman said. "Good luck."

Greer walked CB away and I went to the truck to get my winter jacket to pull over me. This wasn't a good idea, it was dumb because it was so cold.

I caught up with Greer. "Let's go home."

"They haven't pinned the class yet!"

"So." I pulled my winter gloves on over my show gloves. "It's freezing out here. I rode. I didn't make a fool of myself. Mission Accomplished."

Greer shook her head. "Fine. We'll leave. Let's just go back to the indoor and see if the class is over."

"Waste of time," I replied as the three of us trudged back over the frozen driveway.

As soon as we reached the building, the steward waved me over. "We've been calling your number."

"I already rode," I said.

"To be pinned. Didn't you hear it on the PA system?"

"No, the wind is blowing in my ears," I replied.

"Get on!" Greer pulled off the cooler and gave me a leg up.

I entered the ring to find five other horses already inside.

"First Place goes to Talia Margolin on Bittersweet Farm's Fred...Froo..Gist? Something," the announcer said over the loudspeaker.

The crowd laughed. I burst into laughter and threw my arms around his neck.

Greer ran into the ring as the blue ribbon was hooked on his browband. "Sit up!" She took the picture.

We left the ring, she took the cooler from the person she had thrown it to and we put it back on CB.

"Did that prove anything to you?" Greer asked.

"That we make a good team."

"You and CB."

"And you."

My phone began ringing. "Who now?" I checked it. Lockie. I clicked it on.

"Hi!"

"Greer sent me the photo. You can't imagine how proud I am of you."

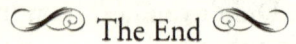 The End

If you love a book, tell a friend.

Sign up for our mailing list and be among the first to know when the next Bittersweet Farm book is released. Send your email address to:
barbara@barbaramorgenroth.com

Note: All email addresses are strictly confidential and used only to notify of new releases.

About the Author

Barbara got her first horse, Country Squire, when she was eleven years old and considers herself lucky to have spent at least as much time on him as she did in the dirt. Next came Yankee Doodle who was far more cooperative and patient with her. Over the years, she showed in equitation classes, hunter classes, went on hunter paces, taught horseback riding at her stable called Sunshine Farm, and went fox hunting on an Appaloosa who would jump anything. With her Dutch Warmblood, Barbara began eventing and again found herself on a horse with great patience and who definitely taught her everything important she knows about horses.